CRAFTING MAGICK
WITH PEN AND INK

ABOUT THE AUTHOR

Susan Pesznecker (Oregon) teaches writing at Portland State University and Clackamas Community College.

TO WRITE TO THE AUTHOR

If you wish to contact the author or would like more information about this book, please write to the author in care of Llewellyn Worldwide and we will forward your request. Both the author and publisher appreciate hearing from you and learning of your enjoyment of this book and how it has helped you. Llewellyn Worldwide cannot guarantee that every letter written to the author can be answered, but all will be forwarded. Please write to:

Susan Pesznecker
c/o Llewellyn Worldwide
2143 Wooddale Drive
Woodbury, MN 55125-2989

Please enclose a self-addressed stamped envelope for reply,
or $1.00 to cover costs. If outside U.S.A., enclose
international postal reply coupon.

Many of Llewellyn's authors have websites with additional information and resources. For more information, please visit our website at www.llewellyn.com

CRAFTING MAGICK
WITH PEN AND INK

Learn to Write Stories, Spells and Other Magickal Works

SUSAN PESZNECKER

FOREWORD BY
RICHARD WEBSTER

Llewellyn Publications
Woodbury, Minnesota

First Edition
Fourth Printing, 2016
Cover design and illustration by Kevin R. Brown
Background leaf image © Brand X Pictures
Interior book design by Joanna Willis
Editing by Mindy Keskinen and Nicole Edman
Llewellyn is a registered trademark of Llewellyn Worldwide Ltd.

Library of Congress Cataloging-in-Publication Data
Pesznecker, Susan Moonwriter
  Crafting magick with pen and ink : learn to write stories, spells, and other magickal works / by Susan Pesznecker. — 1st ed.
      p. cm.
  ISBN 978-0-7387-1145-4
  1. Magic—Authorship. I. Title.
  BF1621.P44 2009
  133.4'3—dc22
                                                                                          2008046408

Llewellyn Publications
A Division of Llewellyn Worldwide Ltd.
2143 Wooddale Drive
Woodbury, MN 55125-2989
www.llewellyn.com

Printed in the United States of America

This work is dedicated to my magickal companion and spirit-familiar Ernie, for his unfailing devotion. More than anyone else, he was with me every step of the way as this work took shape. He departed for the poodle Summerlands on May 2, 2007. May his tail always wag. Zub zub, Ernie . . .

CONTENTS

FOREWORD

When I was a teenager, a friend and I performed a small ritual together. We each wrote a letter, which we placed in envelopes and burned to send our requests out into the universe. I was slightly skeptical about the whole procedure and didn't give it much thought. A couple of weeks later, I realized my request had been granted. My friend also experienced success. This modest beginning set me on a lifelong exploration of just how powerful the combination of writing and magick can be.

Over the years, I have experimented with many ideas that combine writing and magick. Some worked extremely well; others sounded good in theory but yielded mixed results. I vividly remember climbing a hill near my home holding a paper airplane on which I had written my request in invisible ink. It was daybreak, and the air was crisp and cool. I stood on top of the hill, thought about my request and my intense desire for it and threw the paper plane. It soared beautifully, but almost as soon as I'd released it, the thought occurred to me that my dart would ultimately create litter on this beautiful hill. I spent several minutes chasing it all the way down to the bottom of the hill. After a lengthy, graceful flight—which I would have enjoyed watching at any other time—my dart landed on the frost-covered grass. I grabbed it, scrunched it into a ball, and returned home. My request was eventually granted, but only after I'd repeated it using another, litter-free method. I obviously needed this book many, many years ago. Unfortunately, at that time, nothing like it was available.

I've been involved with both writing and magick for many decades. Before reading Sue Pesznecker's book, I thought I knew almost all there was to know about combining the two subjects. I was wrong. Sue knows an amazing amount about both writing and magick, and she explains it all clearly and entertainingly. By the time I'd finished reading this book, I'd learned a great deal and made major changes to the way I do my journaling, spellwork, and preparation of rituals. Sue is an excellent teacher, and her enthusiasm and expertise shine through every page.

With the help of this book, you'll avoid many of the mistakes I made. Your writing and magickal skills will expand and grow. You'll also become more effective, and much more powerful, in both writing and magick. You'll be a true magickal writer.

Richard Webster

PREFACE

By a happy stroke of fate, I was born into a family of magick practitioners. My grandmother and the generations of women who preceded her were accomplished herbalists, wise women practicing eastern European leechcraft, a tradition of medicinal herbology passed from one generation to the next. My mother recalls a childhood filled with regular doses of spring tonics and home remedies, potions hand-crafted in a time when the nearest physician was a day's ride away and the women knew that their methods were better anyway. Mom was always highly in tune with earthly magick; as a young child I often heard Mom proclaim herself a Pagan Sunworshipper. We spent summer weekends camping beside mountain lakes where she worked as a swim teacher and lifeguard, standing wide-legged as her eyes skimmed the water, her body strong and oiled and deeply tanned under the hot sun, a stern goddess in bandana with a whistle, a zinc-coated nose, and a voice that carried over the lake. Magick also comes to me through my father's side, where I'm linked by lineage and geography to people who practiced Scottish Wicca, Pictish magick, and Celtic Druidry; I'm also linked to medicine lines from the Nez Perce nation. Magickal tools and totems have found me across the generations: my grandmother's rolling pin, quill pens, and small iron cauldron; my father's genealogy texts; a family cookbook with remedies and tonics penciled into the page margins; and the talisman of talismans, the family watermelon rock.

I was also born into a family of writers with a heritage of journals and diaries and books, of poems and stories, scrapbooks and sketches, recipe cards, birthday messages, and treasured letters with violets pressed between the pages. My grandmother left me the journals she kept on train and pioneer wagon journeys westward to Oregon, pages filled with dreams and inspirations. She loved to write poems and would walk along the banks of the Columbia River with pen and tablet, pausing now and then to draft a few lines, toes stirring ideas in the cool, living water. My mother commemorated significant family events with letters, and she wrote in a personal journal every evening until her hand was stopped by a stroke in 2006. My father was a pioneer television journalist in Washington and Idaho, and through his lineage I'm able to count the late anchor, Chet Huntley, as my great-uncle. All three of my children write—the two oldest are journalists, and my bookend daughters hoard boxes of spiral notebooks filled with stories, thoughts, and secret moments that date back to their girlhoods.

Today I am a Hearth Pagan and practitioner of green magick, as well as a writer, writing teacher, nurse, mother, and fourth-generation Oregonian, not necessarily in that order. I teach writing at Clackamas Community College and Portland State University (both in Oregon) and also teach magick and wizardry (and magickal writing) to students through the online Grey School of Wizardry. I love to read, work in my herb garden, go rockhounding, and find any possible reason to be outdoors. Life is the best—many blessings!

I offer thanks to my mother, because if it weren't for her, I wouldn't be here. Abiding love also goes to my family, my children, my friends, and the many writers and teachers among them. I am thankful for the gifts of words that have come to me through time and blood.

This book was first crafted as I finished the nonfiction MA writing program at Portland State University. My advisor, Debra Gwartney, proved invaluable in editing this book and making critical suggestions that improved its content and structure, and I honor her tireless and patient support. I am also grateful for the critical eye of Meryl Lipman over a long winter and spring of Wednesday evening sessions. Thanks also go to my graduate committee—Debra Gwartney, Hildy Miller, Susan Reese, Katy Barber, and Frodo Okulam—and to Michael McGregor, for accepting me into the writing program at PSU and for seeming to think he could make a writer out of me. And Bob Hamm, you didn't think I'd forget you, did you?

A wave of the wand sends motes of writer-dust to my magickal community—especially Elizabeth Barrette, Crow Dragontree, Oberon Zell-Ravenheart, Stacey Sherwood, Jymi x/0 ("x divided by zero"), and Oranstar—each of whom provided support and encouragement at the right moments.

Finally, a heartfelt thanks to my students, both in writing and in magick, who have taught me things I couldn't otherwise have learned. Becoming a teacher has been one of the joys of my life.

Ex animo.

INTRODUCTION

Hail and welcome to all whose paths have led to the pages of this book! If you're here, you're probably a magickal practitioner of some sort. You might be eclectic or you might follow an established tradition; you might honor four elements, seven, or none; you might worship the sun or the moon; you might be seer, lorekeeper, or spellcaster; you might be solitary or a member of a robust and thriving circle. Regardless of tradition, what connects all magickal practitioners is the practice of magick itself. Magick is craft, an intentional activity in which we use our hands-on skills to create something unique. As with any undertaking, our ability to work magick improves with study and practice—and with increasing expertise comes an even greater thirst for understanding and mastery. It's one of those wonderful examples of expanding energy: the more you know, the more there is to know, and the more you *want* to know.

But this is a book about writing . . . and what does writing have to do with magick?

The answer: everything.

If you're new to the magickal world, you've probably acquired much of your knowledge through books, which means you've studied the written experiences of your fellow magickal practitioners. You may have undergone in-person mentoring or apprenticeship, with lessons revealed from a grimoire, Book of Shadows, or other document kept and guarded by a circle or coven. You've likely kept records of your own spells, rituals, or herbal workings, and you've almost certainly worked with journaling. If you possess a strong creative streak, you may have tried your hand at writing magickal poetry or stories. If you're more of a scholar-journalist, perhaps you've wished for the skills to produce a publishable essay or magazine piece. You may already be a writer, looking for ways to stretch and improve. Like magick, writing is a craft: it takes intention and skill, and we do it with our own hands, fueled by the power and vitality that drives our souls.

I'm approaching my third decade of magickal practice, and for me, these two worlds have become almost inseparable. What is writing, after all, if not magick? A scribe picks up a pen (or sets fingers to a keyboard) and transmits intangible thoughts, ideas, and perceptions into symbols on a page. Something ethereal seeps from the imagination into the plane of reality, where it takes on a life of its own. Once formed, letters and words are heavy with substance and purport and intention, not only in literal terms but in their human history; the very act of writing forges new links in an ancient chain. Humans have used the tools of their times—mud tablets, quills, fountain pens, laptops—to engage in the task of creating symbols that move readers to emotion and inspiration, even to dreams. Even more remarkably, our fellow humans can pick up our writing, read it, and learn.

At its heart, to write is to communicate, and in today's electronic world, people are drawn to all kinds of writing as both a means of expression and a kind of craft. Magickal followers may feel this thirst more deeply than most: they need a vehicle for self-expression and communication, a means of study, and a way to document and spread magickal traditions and spiritual practices. Writing gives voice to experienced practitioners and helps bring new members into the fold. In an era that commonly dismisses magick as fantasy and superstition, writing provides a focus of community and an oasis for seekers. Even more important, writing provides a way to develop and express both spirituality and magickal craft. Pagan, Druid, Wiccan, and other "earth-based" traditions are among the fastest-growing spiritual practices in the United States today, and one has only to look at bookstores' expanding shelf space for these topics or the growth in "New Age" shops in small towns to understand how true this is. Most cities and towns in the United States have growing magickal communities, with newsletters and directories matching practitioners with groups and seekers with teachers. Today's magickal practitioners yearn to share and learn from each other, and the craft of writing is helping the craft of magick to grow and thrive.

Whatever your writing interests, you'll find guidance and suggestions in this book. Are you interested in keeping a nature journal? Starting a Book of Shadows? Creating guided meditations, spells, or rituals? Writing a piece for your coven newsletter, or perhaps a work of fantasy fiction? You're in the right place. If you're a beginning writer, this book will introduce you to the elements of the craft, helping you generate ideas and develop them with skill. Think back to when you learned to work magick: you didn't just grab a cauldron and some incense and a couple of candles and go to it. First there was a lot to learn about magickal ethics and the importance of intention, about correspondences, gathering materials, the mental arts, and much more. You studied each of these components and then proceeded to compose your first start-to-finish spell. Writing is no different: there are steps to master, and if you take the time to learn them well, your writing will be that much stronger and more effective—just as with magick.

If you consider yourself a novice or beginning writer, I suggest you read the book from beginning to end. Each chapter springs from the one before it, teaching mechanics and structure and concluding with exercises to strengthen and connect your magickal and writing crafts. These "Scribbulus" exercises build on each other, and if you do them in order, your writing skills will grow with each chapter.

On the other hand, if you're an experienced writer looking for specific guidelines—for example, how to shape a ritual or start a short story—you might want to skip ahead to the chapters that catch your interest. However, I'd still encourage you to look through the rest of the book and try out the writing exercises: some will be new to you, and others will revive ideas that you may not have practiced for some time.

You'll also see sidebars throughout this book. The "Magickal Mention"s will help you build your magickal lexicon and knowledge toolkit, and the "Writer's Grimoire" tips will help you better understand some of the finer points of writing.

As you traverse this book, you'll work your way through the art and craft of magickal writing, developing ways to support your magickal workings and enrich your spiritual growth. At the end, we'll invoke the power of the moon through the ritual of Drawing Down the Moon, only this time, we'll be "Writing Down the Moon," urging that ethereal, bottomless well of muse and magick to flow through our bodies and pens, connecting us with an unceasing flow of words. The force is with us, and the magickal powers of the universe are unfailing. Send your magick out into the cosmos through your writing and that magick will return many times over. Bright blessings!

NOTES ON WORD USAGE

- The spelling of "magick" indicates a spiritual or arcane practice, as distinct from "magic," which refers to a sleight-of-hand conjury performed by a professional or parlor magician.

- The acronyms BCE ("before the common era") and CE ("common era") are used here to replace BC and AD (usually taken to mean "before Christ" and "*Anno Domini*," or "the year of our Lord").

- To assure gender-neutral language, the pronouns *she* and *he* are used alternately whenever possible.

one

WHY WRITE?

Why are humans moved to write? We write to communicate, to share ideas, to respond to our thoughts and feelings, to interact with the world. We express opinions. We tell stories. We pour out our souls. As students or apprentices, we engage with our subject matter through writing. Whether we scribble in the margins of a book, scratch out an infusion recipe on an index card, or add material to a Book of Shadows, writing is a tool that helps us expand our view. Writing can even change the world: consider the effects of Martin Luther's ninety-five theses tacked to the door of Wittenberg's Castle Church in 1517, or the impact of Starhawk's 1979 *Spiral Dance*, which set the magickal world on its pointy ears.

In modern times, learning to write has marked the passage from babyhood into childhood, with cursive penmanship likewise marking the transition from childhood into preadolescence. When I think back to grade school, I remember hours of penmanship classes, letters traced and retraced on lined tablets under Mrs. Simon's steady gaze. In the primary years, we'd gotten by with block printing, but promotion to fourth grade meant learning the mysteries of cursive handwriting, with ink pens and heavy paper replacing pencils and pencil tablets. The excitement wore off when we realized that, even though we were now cool fourth graders who could write in cursive, the hours of practice time had doubled, eating into recess and outweighing any immediate benefits.

Today's schoolchildren still endure writing drills, but I know from my own children that long hours of penmanship are a thing of the past, and that many of those hours have been replaced with keyboarding classes, beginning in the primary grades. Today we're more apt to keep in touch with friends by text messaging, e-mailing, or instant messaging than by penning a letter. We keep blogs and social networking Web pages and send electronic animated greeting cards on special occasions. Literary historians ponder what will happen in years to come when the once-standard authorial collections of papers, correspondence, and documents have disappeared entirely, replaced by files and storage media. More and more newspapers, magazines, and books are available electronically, and even the publishing industry is shifting to electronic forms, electronic self-publishing, and cyber "fishbowls" in which writers and poets share their work over the Internet.

Yet even as the electronic age pulls us away from pen and paper, the physical art of writing continues to hold appeal. The act of writing is simple, self-contained, and aesthetic. There is something satisfying about writing on heavy parchment with a silver fountain pen or colorful gel inks; there is pleasure in running fingers over textured papers or reading words set in a flowing hand. But whether we work on screen or on paper, writing is a visible manifestation of spoken language, a use of symbols—alphabets, images, sigils, annotations—to represent words and convey meaning. Through writing, our ideas take on weight. Through writing, we share information with other humans and document ourselves for some sort of imagined posterity. Writing sparks a connection that defies time, a link of recall that surges to the surface when we read notes in the margins of an old family cookbook or a photo album captioned by hand. We're electrified by the idea that we can create something tangible, something unique that outlasts us, transcending a single lifespan to be read by future generations. We write because it gives us pleasure to do so, because it allows us to think and create and study and interact, putting a bit of ourselves onto the page in a way that forges a personal link with the past and the future.

As magickal practitioners, we have an extra advantage in that we view writing as an inherently magickal act. We write in magickal journals, add to herbal formularies, and jot down details of spellcraft and ritual. We study arcane alphabets, and if we still do much of our magickal writing by hand, it's probably linked to our love of the mystical and esoteric. Paper and ink are still "of the earth," and writing by hand is the "old way," the true way, as was done in millennia past. Writing by hand reminds us of medieval monks bent over parchment with ink bottle and quill, of medicine women setting secret formulas to paper by lamplight, or even of ancient Sumerian scribes wielding sticks and mud tablets. Writing gives us a way to set down stories, which create community when shared in story circles and magickal gatherings. Writing by hand feels authentic, especially when we work with quill and ink or an ancient alphabet. It feels necessary, essential, accomplished. In the end, most of us write because we *must*, the act fulfilling a need that can't be met any other way.

WRITING GENRES

When we learn any new skill, we learn about its forms and components. Engage in magick, and you may find yourself practicing Wicca, Druidry, or any of a variety of eclectic variations. Engage in writing and you'll encounter the terms *prose*, *drama*, and *poetry*—the three main genres. The most common by far is prose, which the

American Heritage Dictionary defines as "ordinary speech or writing, without metrical structure." Prose may be as unstructured as a personal journal, as creative as a work of fantasy fiction, or as complex and organized as a Book of Shadows or magickal grimoire. Writers use structural and craft elements to shape, shift, and polish words, yielding a finished piece of writing that may share beliefs, teach, or even entertain.

Writers often define prose in terms of academic versus creative. Academic writing is formal in structure and aims to teach. When we read Buckland's Big Blue Book (*Buckland's Complete Book of Witchcraft*), a handbook of skywatching, or a hard news journalism piece, we're reading to learn. In contrast, creative writing is distinguished by descriptive, imaginative language that aims to "show" rather than just "tell." The word *imagine* comes from the Latin verb *imaginare*, "to form an image or representation of an idea," and when we write creatively, we engage with imagination, transferring visually rich thoughts and ideas onto the page. Such tools as descriptive imagery, simile, and metaphor help make creative prose innovative, expressive, even artistic. That's not to say that academic writing can't also be gorgeous. In fact, the more one practices the craft of writing, the more the lines blur between the various forms.

✒ᴍᴀɢɪᴄᴋᴀʟ
ᴍᴇɴᴛɪᴏɴ

A grimoire (from the French *grammaire*, "grammar") is a how-to book of magickal spells, traditions, and inspirations. A Book of Shadows is a collection of personal spells, rituals, correspondences, and other magickal resources.

And that's part of the fun: master some tasks and techniques, and they'll serve you well, crossing thresholds between poetry, ritual, journaling, or even a letter to a long-lost friend.

Prose encompasses both fiction and nonfiction. Fiction, deriving from the Latin *fingere*, "to form or contrive," is original writing that describes imaginary characters, places, and events (or occasionally uses real or historic settings and figures). Nonfiction writing centers on real people, settings, and events. Some types of creative nonfiction—such as memoir and personal essay—qualify as personal narratives: that is, they tell a personal story.

For our purposes in this book, we'll consider a personal subcategory of prose that lends itself to magick users: *sub rosa* writing. The term is Latin for "under the rose," a Templar emblem of secrecy and privacy. *Sub rosa* work envelops such intimate forms of narrative writing as journaling and reflecting, as well as magickal applications such as spellcrafting and the creation of personal grimoires and Books of Shadows. These types of writing are personal and usually not intended to be read or used by others. But they're important in magick-specific writing—ritual, spellcraft, chant, and so on—and are invaluable in developing one's magickal practices.

Can people be taught to work magick? Absolutely. Can they be taught to write? Most people—myself included—believe that while the muses only inspire a limited number of Faulkners, Prousts, Bucklands, or Starhawks, all of us can find both purpose and pleasure in writing, and anyone can be taught to write with more fluency, clarity, and enjoyment. That's the first task of this book: teaching you, magickal reader, more about writing as craft. This book aims to bring you, writing, and magick closer together. Writing is an intimate, personal experience, and the very act inspires self-exploration. Since self-exploration and self-knowledge are hallmarks of magickal and spiritual practice, it's a short stretch to envision writing as a natural extension of magick, and to understand that one enriches the other. The writer who begins with journaling may progress to writing essays for an online magickal e-zine, or to story-crafting for the next Bardic circle. Work good magick, and you'll find reasons to write about it; write about your magickal workings, and you'll find yourself immersed in reflection, strengthening your magick over time.

This text also has a practical side, for we'll share a number of ways to expand your magickal writing life. At the end of this journey, you'll emerge as a better writer, a better-equipped magick practitioner, and one who has enjoyed the journey.

1. Imagine you're sitting in a Magickal Writing 101 class, and it's your turn to introduce yourself. Write an imagined introduction telling about your experiences with magick and writing and what you hope to gain from the class. Sign the introduction, date it, and set it aside.

2. What's your writing background? What's your first memory of writing? What do you consider to be "good" writing? How has your education or other personal experience influenced your writing ability, for better or worse? Do you have any writing treasures—old family scrapbooks or recipe books? Letter collections? Do you keep a diary or journal? Do you have a favorite author? Write a page or more that depicts a case history of *you*, as a writer. Date this piece as well, and make a habit of dating all of your writings to document your magickal writing life.

two

THE WRITER'S TOOLKIT

<u>*Journal entry, August 23*</u>

It's morning, early—maybe 6:00. The cat is still asleep, but I'm at my desk, working on my journal. Writing. I'm in PJs, a cup of mint-and-hyssop tea next to me. Through the desk-high window to my right, I can see the backyard coming to life, the early birds at the feeders, a breeze rustling through the hawthorn tree, a fading full moon settling down in the west. The words come easily at this time of day—I can type almost as fast as I can think. Ideas rise like the dawn chorus, and if I'm lucky, I'll look up at the clock and find that two hours have slid by and I've written several pages, all while the house dozed and dreamed around me.

Ink and paper in hand (or keyboard under hand), you're ready to begin. Are you excited? You should be—you're about to work magick! Like any epic journey, this one starts at the beginning, and any writing endeavor begins with a simple question: when, where, and how do you write?

Like everyone else, magickal folks operate differently at different times of day, and your identification as morning person or night owl will have a powerful interface with your writing. Ask a dozen writers about their work habits and you'll get a dozen different answers. The morning people might do their best work as the sun comes up, then find that they fall asleep wherever they're sitting at eight in the evening, while the night owls scribble ideas into the wee hours but can't lift a pencil before noon. Depending on your daily schedule, you might squeeze writing into thirty-minute increments captured during lunch hour or after dinner, or you might have the luxury of setting aside one or two hours each day. One writer might be driven by the need to finish a specific task, while the laid-back writer might sit down with no agenda other than freewriting, with no idea where he's headed.

Both approaches are fine—the important thing is to discover what works for you, and then to make space for writing in your everyday life and a place for your tools, processes, and rituals.

WHAT MAKES WRITING EASY? OR HARD?

If you want to be a writer, you have to write. Seems simple enough—yet many people freeze up when faced with a blank sheet of paper or an empty computer screen. The explanations range from "I don't have enough time" to "I don't know what to write," "I can't get started," "I don't understand grammar," "I'm not that creative," and "Back in fifth grade, Mrs. Robinson told me I was a bad writer."

If you identify with any of the above, I'd like you to trot out your own personal list of excuses one final time. You might even formalize the occasion by writing them down (in black ink, of course) and dating the list, then burning it in a thurible with one or more banishing herbs: birch, buckthorn, mint, mistletoe, rosemary, and thistle are some good options. This is your last chance to drag out those old excuses—because I'm here to tell you, promise you, assure you that you *can* write, that you can enjoy it, that it can be fun, and that it can make your magickal and mundane lives richer.

THE WRITER'S TOOLS

One of the niftiest truths about writing is that it's easy and cheap. After all, you only need a pencil and paper to get started. But you'll probably *want* a few more tools: pens or pencils of your choice, one or more journal notebooks, erasers, or—if you prefer working electronically—a good computer. Be sure to think about convenience, because you'll have the best results if your materials are pleasant to use and easy to carry around with you.

Let's begin with journal notebooks. Small journals are portable enough to take anywhere, tucked into purse, pocket, or magick kit. Larger ones are less portable but provide a generous workspace. Spiral or bound notebooks have fixed pages that can't get lost, but also can't be rearranged. Three-ring binders allow you to add various pages and page elements, as well as to move elements around.

Once you've decided on a journal book, you'll need something to write with. Pens—particularly gel pens—are easy to use, and colored or metallic inks can enliven or highlight your writing. For example, you might make nature-oriented entries in green ink, magick entries in purple, and cosmological entries in silver ink on black paper. Some writers adopt a specific ink color as their personal signature. For special occasions, you might invest in a calligraphy or fountain pen—I use a heavy silver pen for lunar magick and rituals. Many magickal supply stores sell quills, or you might make your own. (See Chapter 12 for more on working with quills, scrolls, and inks.)

Some writers prefer pencils for their early drafts. I knew a writer who used pencils exclusively; she kept sharpening and wearing them down until they were two inches long and too small to hold comfortably, at which point she'd toss the stubs into an empty fishbowl on her desk. She loved watching the bowl fill up with her "accomplished" pencils (and it was a great conversation starter, too).

There's a world of special papers available today, and notebook users can also have fun working with papers and scrapbooking techniques. Papers in various colors, textures, designs, and materials are available by the ream or the sheet. Edging (deckling) scissors and shaped hole punches can add cutaways and detailed edgings to your pages.

In today's electronic age, many writers prefer to work with a computer, either desktop or laptop. While some see handwriting as a more pure, authentic kind of practice, others find that the ease of computer use outweighs its modernity. Computers let the writer store, retrieve, rearrange, and revise ideas quickly. Word-processed documents are easy to read—a boon if you're one of those people whose handwriting resembles hieroglyphics—and of course you can adjust font, size, and formatting such as bold and italic text. You can even download special magickal fonts. Today's computers usually come with a built-in dictionary and thesaurus in addition to Internet capabilities.

As you begin writing more regularly, you'll probably mix and match the above approaches, creating your own practice. I'm definitely a hybrid writer. I do most of my own magickal writing on

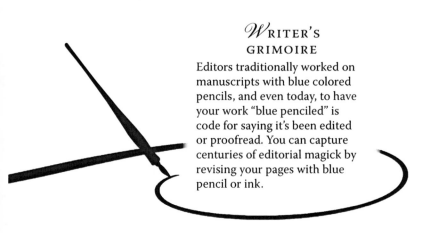

Writer's GRIMOIRE

Editors traditionally worked on manuscripts with blue colored pencils, and even today, to have your work "blue penciled" is code for saying it's been edited or proofread. You can capture centuries of editorial magick by revising your pages with blue pencil or ink.

my laptop, but I also keep small bound scratch journals in my coat pockets and "witchy bag." I use them to jot down ideas that come to me when I'm away from home; when I get home, I transfer the ideas to my laptop, giving the new file a simple name so I can find it quickly in the future. I also keep a hanging file folder for ideas gleaned from newspapers or magazines and for storing pages torn out of my scratch journals.

Collecting and working with different writing materials can be a lot of fun—for some, it becomes a magickal practice in itself. If you're a nature lover and do a lot of your journaling outdoors, check with an outdoor store for "write anywhere" journals and pens that let you take notes in any conditions, from pouring rain to sub-zero temperatures, and even upside down! If most of your work will take place indoors and you love the aesthetic, check your local bookstore or magick shop for hard- and softbound journals, perhaps one with a design that lets you match each journal's form with its function. A journal adorned with a Tree of Life might be a wonderful focus for nature magick. If you intend to keep your journals for a long time—and most of us do—look for paper and covers of archival quality, guaranteed to last hundreds of years or more without deteriorating.

Filling Your Kit

Most of us magick types have some sort of bag or kit in which we organize and haul around our tools, garb, and supplies. My witchy bag happens to be a heavyweight nylon tool bag with a gazillion pockets and dividers, overflowing with everything from wand-making materials to tarot cards to rockhounding tools to a spell-craft pouch of herbs, stones, salt, and candles.

As a writer, you'll create a writer's toolbox, or at least you'll stuff your writing tools into a corner of your magick kit. For the work you'll be doing in this book, I recommend these basic materials:

- a notebook or journal dedicated to magickal writing, as discussed above

- a small sketchbook

- your choice of pens and pencils in two or more colors

- at least one highlighter pen

- a pencil sharpener (or small pocketknife)

- a good eraser

- art supplies as desired (colored pencils, felt pens, gel pens, and so on)

- a set of small self-adhesive notes, for flagging pages in books or in your journal

- a few bookmarks

- a ruler

- index cards (5 × 7 recommended, lined or unlined)

Your Writing Library

A good dictionary is a must for writers. You'll find them in every price range: many are even available online, but I still suggest you keep a "real" dictionary on your desk. Get the biggest one you can afford, and look for one that includes etymologies (word origins). The Holy Grail in this case is the twenty-volume *Oxford English Dictionary*; its $1,500-plus price is beyond the means of most of us, but perhaps with the right abundance spell . . . who knows? Most university libraries have on-shelf and online versions of the OED; if you have access to this resource, rejoice! But for everyday use, my current favorite is the *American Heritage Dictionary of the English Language* (fourth edition). It's illustrated and features detailed etymologies, biographical sketches, maps, charts, and tables. Besides being a great resource, it's also just plain fun to thumb through.

Depending on what and how you write, you may want to add some special references to your shelves. A rhyming dictionary can help with composing chants, poems, or ritual, while a visual dictionary uses detailed images and diagrams to illustrate definitions. A thesaurus helps when you're looking for the perfect word, and a basic grammar text or writer's guide can resolve tricky usage questions. See the Resources section at the end of this book for suggestions on these sources and more.

THE WRITER'S MILIEU

While one of the best things about writing is the flexibility of being able to do it anywhere, it can be wonderful to have a space dedicated to your craft. If you're lucky, you might have a room that you can turn into a dedicated writing nook, but a corner will do. Perhaps you already have a *sanctum sanctorum* for your tools, books, and magickal practice materials, and you can create a small writing area there. You'll want a spot that gives you room to spread out. Include a comfortable chair and a good light source, and keep reference books close by. For a portable option, collect your writing materials in a briefcase or book bag to create instant writing space anywhere you go.

Customize your writing space as desired. You may prefer a quiet environment, or you might find that you work best when surrounded by sound—music or radio, for example. Bach, Mozart, and Gregorian

*M*AGICKAL
MENTION

A *sanctum* (sacred place) or *sanctum sanctorum* (literally, "holy of holies") is a space dedicated to spiritual and magickal practices.

chant are good as background music, as their mathematical integrity allows you to be aware of them without demanding active listening. Celtic music and Native American flutes also make excellent writing backdrops. Use area lighting or a desk lamp to illuminate your workspace. Avoid long-tube fluorescent lights: their spectrum is unhealthy and they tend to issue a subliminal flicker, giving rise to headaches in people susceptible to them. Compact fluorescents are an effective and environmentally responsible lighting option.

Most writers enjoy enhancing their writing area with personal items: photographs, family memorabilia, special writing tools, and so on. The family photos that line your desk, the silver fountain pen used for special occasions, and the mug with WRITER inscribed on its side . . . they all become talismans, anchoring the presence of magick there. These items don't have to be expensive or fancy: the simplest item may be the most powerful for you, provided it holds some sort of memory-link that speaks to you. Bless and consecrate the most special of these items and you will have created a powerful talisman for your writing craft.

Use magickal tools and correspondences to further add to the magickal nature of your setting. We'll talk more about this in chapters to come, but here are some ideas to get you started:

- A quill, shaped and charged under the light of the waxing moon, will inspire your work and prove to be a powerful magickal writing tool.

MAGICKAL
MENTION

A talisman is a sort of magickal storage battery, drawing positive, intentional energy inward toward the practitioner.

- A violet crystal—a piece of amethyst, perhaps—will support perception, intuition, and psychic powers, all paths to strengthening one's writing.

- A candle scented with rosemary essential oils will support your mental powers and perform a magickal cleansing of the workspace each time it's lit.

- A cup of tea brewed from peppermint and thyme will inspire your work and help prevent writer's headache.

Your writing surface is another important aspect of your work area. If you have space for a desk, get the biggest one you can find: it's terrific to have enough room to spread out papers, pens, a laptop, books, and other writerly items.

As a magickal practitioner, you're likely to use your desk as a unique kind of altar space—a place where you work the special magick of writing. As you gather your materials and fill your writing desk-altar with tools and talismans, the magick grows, suffusing your work with energy. Each word you write carries power, your pens and pencils working as symbols that connect you to fellow writers across the millennia, all using different tools but all practicing the same amazing magick: the transfer of ideas and intention into tangible form. At your desk-altar, you open your mind to inspiration and insight, and you enter sacred space.

You may wish to set up a miniature magickal altar on one corner of your desk. I use a glass dish painted with a vivid spiral. On the dish I keep several stones, a small bowl of salt, sea shells, a white candle, and a vial of charged moonwater. These magickal objects sit on the southern corner of my desk, south being the direction of fire and thus echoing the passions I hope to ignite in my writer's heart.

Establishing an Initial Writing Routine

Like any skill, writing requires practice and discipline. If you're going to become better at writing, you have to write every day—or almost every day—and the easiest way to accomplish this is by building time into your schedule. You might begin by writing for fifteen to twenty minutes at about the same time every day. Do this for a week or two, evaluate, and make adjustments. Plan your writing for a time of day when you're alert, productive, and unlikely to be interrupted.

Ergonomics: Mundane and Magickal

Practicing good ergonomics will make your writing environment both efficient and comfortable. Choose a writing chair that's comfortable and provides good back support. With your feet flat on the floor in front of you, your knees should fall just below your seat. If you use a computer, make sure your work surface is at the proper height: you should be able to let your hands hover over the keyboard without having to bend your wrists or prop them on the desk's edge. Ideally, your elbows will form a 90-degree angle when your hands are over the keys. Set the monitor high enough so that when you gaze straight ahead, your eyes contact the upper third of the screen; this minimizes strain on eyes and neck. Following these alignments will keep you comfy and help avoid stress to arms, wrists, and neck.

When you sink into a writing project, minutes and hours can pass without your realizing it. Sitting in one position for long periods is hard on the joints and muscles and slows circulation in the legs, so aim to take breaks every half hour or so. Stand up, bend your knees a few times, stretch and flex your arms and wrists, wiggle your fingers, and so on. Writing with a computer is also hard on the eyes: when staring at a computer screen, we blink less often, which causes the eyes to dry and become uncomfortable. Get into the habit of looking up from the screen every few minutes, blinking

Think of these traditional practices as "magickal ergonomics"
for writers, too.

- *Centering*: the act of focusing
  and gathering your energy and
  intentions in your body's center. For most people, this is the
  area just behind the navel.

- *Grounding*: the act of connecting your own energy with that
  of the Earth.

- *Meditation*: the act of moving
  intentionally from a state of
  active engagement with one's
  surroundings into a waking
  state of focus and calm.

- *Visualization*: imagining a
  place, thing, person, or process
  in a focused way—for example, a wildflower meadow
  or a burning candle flame.
  The act of visualizing actually
  uses several senses: you may
  see, hear, smell, and "feel" the
  candle flame in your mind's
  eye. Visualization is one way to
  achieve a meditative state.

several times, and focusing on something far away, something close up, and something far away again. This gives your eyes their own mini-calisthenic break. If you can work next to a window, so much the better: you'll have something to look at, and the view will provide a constant source of inspiration and ideas.

Anyone who has worked with magick knows what a magickal hangover feels like and will agree the experience is best avoided. As a magickal writer, you must deal with energy that is manifested or manipulated; otherwise, a headache, fatigue, or general sludgy feeling results. Using meditation or visualization at the beginning of a writing session will help you focus the energies needed for the work, and a moment of centering will help gather and intensify your creative forces. Grounding at the end of a magickal writing session allows unused energies to return to the universe's creative wellspring, ready to be dipped back into at a later time, but freeing you from the hangover caused by bits and dabs of chaotic, unused voltage. You might even try visualizing a well, or maybe even an earthly file cabinet, into which those ideas and impulses are grounded (filed) for later access.

MAKING A MAGICKAL WRITER'S STOLE

Most of us don't don magickal robes and regalia for every writing session. As an alternative, I'd like to suggest a writer's stole: it's easy to make and is just the thing to empower your writing intentions.

You'll need:
- a piece of cloth 30 to 36 inches wide and a few inches longer than your outstretched arms from fingertip to fingertip

- straight pins

- an iron

- matching thread and a sewing machine—or, for threadless hemming, some fusible webbing or seam binding (see step 6 below)

Step by step:

1. Choose fabric in a color and pattern that reflects your magickal interests. If the fabric is washable, pre-wash it and dry it before beginning. Use your scissors to trim away any frayed edges.

2. Making the stole is as simple as hemming all four sides. Start by turning all four edges under about ¼ inch toward the fabric's wrong side, and then ironing each fold into a crease. Use straight pins to hold the fold in place.

3. Now use your sewing machine to stitch the folded edges in place, sewing with the fabric's wrong side facing up. Don't worry if this isn't perfect—it's not going to show in the end.

4. Starting with one of the long sides, fold the stitched edge under again about ⅝ inch (the traditional hem width) and pin the new fold in place. Use your sewing machine to sew the fold closed, with your needle set ½ inch from the fabric's edge (and again, sewing with the wrong side of the fabric facing up).

5. Repeat this with the other long side, then again for the two short sides. Remove any pins and iron all four hems flat and smooth, again with the wrong side facing up. If you are using satin or another exotic material, use a cool iron so you don't burn the fabric.

6. If you don't sew, use fusible webbing or seam binding, available at your local fabric store. These products have a type of glue that melts when ironed, holding fabrics together. Follow the above directions, but omit the stitching. Instead, after folding the hem under ⅝ inch, place thin strips of fusible

webbing under the fold (or place fusible seam binding over its edge) and iron according to directions.

Once it's finished, consecrate or bless the stole to your purposes—then enjoy wrapping it around your shoulders when you invoke your magickal writerly self!

HONORING YOUR BEGINNINGS: A RITUAL

You have your tools, you've created your writing space, and here you are, ready to begin. Let's formalize your beginnings with a ritual. Set aside thirty minutes and arrange a private, quiet place. You'll need a small table or other surface for the ritual items. Your writing space and desk-altar might be perfect! The best time to conduct this ceremony would be at dawn—the time associated with new beginnings and fresh starts—or any time in the morning or afternoon, a time period associated with gathering power.

The ritual outlined here can be adjusted and customized to befit your own traditions. You may wish to have others take part in the ritual with you—this is always your choice.

1. Gather these materials:
   - your writing journal and tools
   - an altarcloth: consider red (for passion and energy), green (creativity and prosperity), or yellow (mental work)
   - symbols of:
       Earth: a graphite pencil and a small dish of salt
       Air: a feather quill (or a plain feather)
       Fire: a red ink pen and a candle
       Water: a bottle of ink, a small dish of water, or both
   - your own personal indications of deity, or a simple white taper for magick and mystery
   - matches
   - a candlesnuffer or silver spoon

- your writer's stole
- "cakes and wine" (that is, a small snack of food and drink)
- additional items of your choice that honor your goals as a writer
- optional: magickal garb and jewelry; a small thurible with a cover and/or some incense of dry, powdered herbs (suggestions: bay, borage, lemongrass, peppermint, rowan, or thyme for strengthening; lemon balm, clover, or ginger for success and inspiration)

2. Spread the altarcloth over the table and set your writing journal and tools in the center. Place the earth symbol above the journal (at 12:00 on an imaginary clock face), the air symbol at 3:00, the fire symbol at 6:00, and the water symbol at 9:00. Place the deity figures or white candle at the far left of the altar and the additional items at the far right. At the near right corner, place your thurible or dish of herbs, if you wish. Place your cakes and wine at the near left. Set the matches and snuffer off to one side.

3. Prop this book open next to the altar space, or take a few notes, if that's all you'll need.

$\mathcal{M}$AGICKAL
MENTION

A thurible is a fireproof container for burning herbs and incense. Small iron cauldrons and large abalone shells are two types of thuribles.

4. Prepare yourself. Wash your hands and face, drying with a clean towel. Slip on your stole or any magickal garb or jewelry. As you prepare, maintain silence, focusing on your initiation into the writer's world.

5. Light the candles. Stand before the altar for two or three minutes, calming yourself and clearing your thoughts. Create an image of yourself writing. Think about the details of what you see.

6. Now, say the following words while carrying out the actions indicated in brackets:

> "**Today I set myself upon the writer's path.**"
>
> "**I ask blessings and strength of earth.** *[Sprinkle a few grains of salt over your writing tools.]* **May vigor and perseverance be mine.**"
>
> "**I ask blessings and strength of air.** *[Waft the feather over your writing tools.]* **May inspiration and mystery be mine.**"
>
> "**I ask blessings and strength of fire.** *[Waft the candle's "smoke" over your writing tools.]* **May passion and creativity be mine.**"
>
> "**I ask blessings and strength of water.** *[Sprinkle a drop or two of water over your writing tools.]* **May energy and transformation be mine.**"
>
> "**May the spirit of the writing craft fill me, gifting me with powers of insight and creation. May the spirit empower my tools, enlivening them to my purpose.**" *[Alternatively, address your own deities as you see fit.]*
>
> *[Light the thurible, if you're using one, then use your hands to waft the smoke over your body; or, if using dry herbs, sprinkle a few over your head.]* "**May the life-power of the herbs bestow their blessing upon me.**"

[Lay hands on writing tools.] "In return for these gifts, I do hereby pledge to honor the crafts of magick and writing, and that I will devote myself to them and will celebrate their traditions and ways."

[Pause for a minute or two of quiet meditation.]

"I bless and release the protection of spirit *[snuff the deity candle]*, water, fire *[snuff the fire candle]*, air, and earth *[snuff other candles and put a lid over the thurible]*. Let us go in peace."

"So mote it be."

7. Pause for a moment of reflection. When you are finished, enjoy your cakes and wine.

Welcome to the craft!

Scribbulus _____

1. Copy the above ritual (or whatever version of it you enacted) into your new writing journal or notebook. You might also want to paste the self-introduction you wrote in Chapter 1 into your journal.

2. What is your ideal writing process? Write a short piece in your journal that explains or describes where and when you write, your favorite materials, and so on. Date the entry. Look back on it every so often—you may find yourself making changes over time.

3. Try out different tools: pens, papers, and so on. Can you develop a sense of which tools feel and work best for you—how about at different times or for different purposes?

4. Establish and follow a simple writing routine for one week, then write a journal entry describing the experience. How well did your routine work? Does the routine need any modifications?

three

ACTS OF CREATION

Whether you're writing a story, crafting a spell, or preparing a set of teaching materials for your coven or circle, every act of writing is an act of creation, and it all begins with ideas. In this chapter, we'll start the magick flowing with activities that help you dip into a hidden well of inspiration and resources. You'll learn techniques for generating ideas—your raw materials—then you'll shape those materials into a draft, and finally, you'll revise and polish your work, probably in several stages.

INVENTION

In the writing world, the term *invention* refers to techniques and exercises that help you spark and develop ideas. Invention work is the wide-open, no-holds-barred, boundary-free writing that taps into the hidden, nearly unconscious creativity that flows through all of us. It also helps you ignore your internal censor, the one that says "wait—you spelled that wrong" or "nobody will want to read that." Use invention for any and all writing activities, whether they are simple or formal, magickal or mundane.

Before You Begin

Prepare yourself by grounding, centering, or engaging in a short meditation. Clear your mind and focus on the task at hand—intent is an important part of both magick and writing. Think about what you hope to accomplish. Take several deep, cleansing breaths, and let your awareness expand.

For now, simply surround yourself with your favorite magickal and writing talismans before you begin. In later chapters, you'll learn about invoking the muse and appealing to your writing patrons.

Brainstorming

Neat word, isn't it? Literally a storm within the brain—I envision a whirling tornado with ideas flying out. To brainstorm, sit down with paper and pencil and list everything that comes to mind: the

*M*AGICKAL
MENTION

When we ground and center, we find a locus of internal quiet and calm—sort of a metaphysical *tabula rasa*, a blank slate. Some people do this by consciously emptying their minds. Others connect with the flow of energy emanating from deep within the earth. One techno-wizard friend of mine envisions the process as a "soft reboot" during which she empties her mind and "restarts."

ideas don't have to be related, nor must they be in any sort of logi-cal order. Just let them come. (Variation: Start with a central idea—a prompt—in mind, and brainstorm anything that comes to mind in response to that prompt.) When your pencil stops, take a look at what's on your paper.

Let's imagine that you were preparing a set of teaching materi-als for your coven's class on the elementals. Based on that prompt, your brainstorming list might look something like this:

Candles	*Salamanders*
Safety	*As above*
Altar space	*So below*
Choosing a candle	*Spirit*
Earth	*Green magick*
Air	*Nature*
Fire	*Stone*
Water	*Flames*
Correspondences	*Waterfalls*
Directions	*Sacred space*
Sylphs	*Zodiac*
Undines	*Astrology*
Gnomes	*Passion*

You're off to a fine start here, with lots of ideas. In order to ex-pand those ideas, we'll move on to another kind of invention: free-writing.

Freewriting

Freewriting is a magickal process that circumvents the conscious brain and allows you to access thoughts and ideas you might other-wise have been unaware of. When you freewrite, you write without stopping for a set period of time. You can begin with a prompt, or you can write about nothing in particular. Either way, it's important to keep writing (don't stop!) without censoring yourself—no fair scratching out words, correcting misspellings, or fixing punctuation. Just write whatever comes to mind.

How to do a freewrite

1. If desired, choose a prompt, perhaps from a brainstorming exercise. Here are a few prompts:
   - You're at a public solstice ritual.
   - You're working with a set of runes.
   - You're walking through a forest.

2. Set a timer for five to ten minutes.

3. Start writing and write continuously until the timer sounds. Write whatever comes to mind. If your thoughts stop coming, keep the pencil moving by tracing spirals or writing a word of your choice over and over. The important rules are not to stop and not to censor yourself in any way. The more fluid and uninhibited the writing, the better the result.

4. When the timer sounds, read through your work and underline the ideas that seem interesting. Reflect on how you might expand them into a piece of writing.

Magickal Mention

For magickal folk, freewriting can function as a kind of intuitive divination. When you freewrite, you'll find yourself tapping into your unprotected inner thoughts and awareness. You can even freewrite as an *intentional* part of a divinatory ritual or practice. Whether your divinatory freewriting is spontaneous or ritualized, allow time to reflect on the meaning when you're finished.

Let's look back at the earlier brainstorming list. Imagine that you decided to use the terms "earth" and "stone" as prompts in a quick guided freewrite:

> *Stone is probably one of the best representatives of the earth element, at least for natural or green magick. Stones are everywhere. Easy to find. Cheap to buy. What's the difference between stones, rocks, and crystals? Stones must be cleansed, charged, and blessed before using. Proper storage and periodic recharging required. Consider stones required for a basic stone set. Stones as talismans, altar items. Different stones (igneous, metamorphic, etc.) as congruent to specific elements.*

This is a solid piece of freewriting, full of thoughts and ideas running free and uncensored. You've created the raw materials for a meaningful piece of writing.

Clustering

Another useful form of invention is clustering. Sometimes called mapping, webbing, spidering, or ballooning, clustering is a good way to break a big idea into smaller, more manageable topics, and also to reveal ideas you might not otherwise have thought about. Clustering is especially good for writers who are highly visual.

How to do a clustering activity

1. Write a major idea, question, or prompt in the middle of a page and circle it.

2. What does that major idea or question make you think of? Write that thought close to the original idea, circle it, and draw a line between the two.

3. Keep adding new responses, each time circling the thought and drawing lines between all the circles that relate to one another.

$\mathcal{W}$RITER'S GRIMOIRE

How do you know if you're a visual person? Answer yes or no to these questions:

- Are you more apt to remember what you see, rather than what you read or hear about?

- Do you notice and recall visual details?

- Are you a good judge of dimensions, such as length and weight?

- Do you know—just by looking—how many people can be seated comfortably at a table?

- Do you have a strong, innate sense of direction?

- Can you distinguish between close shades of one color?

If you answered yes to at least four of the above questions, you are extra-attuned to visual learning and memory.

4. Continue the process for as long as you can, until you're out of ideas. Then stop and look over the results. You may identify a key idea, one that connects to many or most of the others. Or, you might find that a group of connected circles in one corner looks interesting.

Freewriting and clustering are complementary. An interesting word, phrase, or idea from freewriting may serve as a great start for a cluster. Or a fascinating point on a cluster-map might provide a prompt for freewriting.

Looping

Looping is a great way to refine or focus an idea. Looping begins with freewriting, then narrows the central idea, condensing it to a more manageable size. Think of freewriting as chemistry: when you freewrite, you empty a slurry of ideas and thoughts into the wide mouth of a funnel. Looping helps you refine and filter the ideas, transforming them into the clarified essence of words and ideas that drip out through the spout at the bottom.

How to use looping

1. Set the timer and freewrite for five to ten minutes.

2. When the timer sounds, stop and read what you've written. Take your pen and underline what you think is the single most interesting or striking idea on the page. As an example, let's look at our earlier freewrite, imagining what we might choose as the most evocative thought:

    > *Stone is probably one of the best representatives of the earth element, at least for natural or green magick. Stones are everywhere. Easy to find. Cheap to buy. What's the difference between stones, rocks, and crystals? Stones must be cleansed, charged, and blessed before using. Proper storage and periodic recharging required. <u>Consider stones required for a basic stone set.</u> Stones as talismans, altar items. Different stones (igneous, metamorphic, etc.) as congruent to specific elements.*

3. Now, set the timer for another five-to-ten-minute freewrite, focusing on the sentence or thought you underlined in step 2 (in this case, "Consider stones required for a basic stone set"). In other words, that thought serves as your new writing prompt.

4. When the timer sounds, stop and read what you've just written. Take your pen and once again underline what you

think is the single most interesting or striking idea in the second freewrite.

> *Consider stones required for a basic stone set. A beginning stone set for new magick users should include fluorite—enhances psychic skills and opens communication channels; amethyst—banishes fear and anxiety, absorbs negativity; psychic qualities (wisdom and purity of thought); bloodstone—heals wounds, averts misfortune; hematite—supports alertness, divination, and scrying; jade—love; life; relationships; quartz points—energy, enthusiasm, strength; rose quartz—healing, calm, and balance; snowflake obsidian—powerful divination stone; Tiger Eye—protects against evil; <u>turquoise—clarity, purification; tranquility, protection against psychic attack (one of the most powerful stones).</u>*

5. Now (I'll bet you've guessed what comes next), freewrite for another five to ten minutes, focusing on the sentence or thought you just underlined, in this case "Turquoise—clarity, purification; tranquility, protection against psychic attack (one of the most powerful stones)."

> *Turquoise—clarity, purification; tranquility, protection against psychic attack (one of the most powerful stones). For its sense of calm and tranquility—important after a long study session or when preparing for an exam or test. Shape of stone, whether rough or polished, etc. Care of turquoise carved as animal fetish. Means of cleansing, charging, etc. Storing. <u>Aligns chakras.</u> Good for referencing the air element.*

Repeat this process as many times as you need to. When should you stop? Stop when the last idea or thought that tumbles out the bottom is the one you want to write about. If you look back through the prompts you selected after each loop, you'll probably find that where you ended up is really different from where you started. Fascinating, isn't it? This is looping at its finest: an idea is magickally changed and shaped until its essence emerges at the end, transformed.

Visual Tricks

The above invention strategies focus on written techniques, but there may be times when "visual invention" will be just what you need. Images can bring new concepts to mind, perhaps "priming the pump" for generating ideas via words. For example:

- Rather than freewriting, experiment with "free-drawing." Use an idea or prompt and sketch whatever comes to mind.

- Work with diagrams, maps, and so on. Drawing a diagram can help you visualize the flow of an essay or a plot line. A map might help you create the outlines of a fictional world.

- Try a collage. Find some paper, glue, and magazines. Cut out words, images, and other symbols from the magazines and glue onto a sheet of paper in whatever manner or design pleases you. See what inspirations surface in the process.

*W*RITER'S
GRIMOIRE

For maximum creativity, approach the process when you're alert and well rested. Eat lightly; high-fat or large meals tend to create mental sludge. Munch a handful of blueberries or some pomegranate seeds, both full of antioxidants and known to be potent memory boosters. (See Chapter 5 for more information on memory work.)

- Some people find that the act of applying color to paper is a meditative process, often yielding new insights. Use crayons or colored pencils for unstructured coloring, or fill in a coloring book or a book of mandala patterns. Take notes of your ideas as they occur.

What Should You Do with Your Invention Work?

Invention can help you in two significant ways. First, as you've seen above, it helps generate and develop ideas. Second, it's a valuable practice tool: think of it as writer's calisthenics that help you tone and build your writing muscles. You might get into the practice of opening every writing session with five to ten minutes of freewriting, just to loosen up.

Some people—I'm among them—save all or most of their invention, having found that much of it contains kernels of ideas that will later grow into larger work. A few writers throw away some or all of their invention work, feeling that the acts of creation and generation are the most important parts of the process, and that what's on the page is less critical than the simple act of setting words on paper. Either approach is valid, but for those who are new to the idea of invention or are approaching serious writing for the first time,

*M*AGICKAL MENTION

A mandala is a geometric figure—usually circular—representing the universe in Hindu and Buddhist symbolism. The same motif appears in other kinds of magick, including Pennsylvania-Dutch hex magick, aboriginal medicine wheels, and the magick circle.

I recommend that you save your work—at least for now. Treat the products of your freewriting and clustering and looping as bits of magickal wisdom, each with a story to whisper in your ear.

FROM INVENTION TO DRAFT

You've done your invention, you have a topic, and now you're ready to organize your ideas into a piece of writing. How do we move from casual, unstructured writing to something with more form and purpose?

Start by organizing your ideas with a simple list or outline. Let's look back at our earlier invention work. Perhaps we thought about what we wanted the introductory elemental class to include, and came up with this simple list:

Introduction: earth element and stones
Definition of stones (rocks, minerals, crystals, etc.)
Where to find or purchase
Cleansing, charging, and blessing stones
A basic stone set for new magick practitioners
Influence of stones' shape, polish, etc.
Using stones on the altar
Using stones for chakra balancing
Using stone as talismans
Storing stones
Conclusion and practice tasks
Tests for mastery

Some writers like working with lists, but others are more comfortable with outlines. Here is the same information, arranged in outline format:

I. Introduction: the earth element and stones

II. Definition of stones
   a. Rocks
   b. Minerals
   c. Crystals
   d. Others

III. Where to find or purchase

IV. Handling Your Stones
   a. Cleansing
   b. Charging
   c. Blessing
   d. Storing

V. A basic stone set for new magick practitioners

VI. Influence of attributes
   a. Stones' shape
   b. Polish or shininess
   c. Other

VII. Uses of Stones
   a. On the altar
   b. Chakra balancing
   c. Talismans

VIII. Practice tasks

IX. Tests for mastery

At this point, you could sit down with a cup of tea and use this list to rough out an essay to use in your coven's class. Begin with a few lines of introduction to the topic, then work through the rest of your outline or list. Devote a paragraph to each of the main ideas, explaining each point carefully. It's always important to consider your audience; if you're writing for readers who know little or nothing about your topic, you'll have to go more slowly and explain in more detail than if you were writing for seasoned experts. Finish with a concluding paragraph that summarizes what you've covered and leaves your reader thinking about what they've read and why it might be important. Don't forget to add a title: odd as it may seem, it's usually easier to create a title after you've written the piece than when you're beginning it. Once you have a first draft down on paper, set it aside for two or three days, then pick it up, reread it, and prepare to enter into the process of revision (see the next section).

A few writers don't make any organizational notes at all: they just start writing. I'm one of those—I spend a few minutes thinking about my central idea and what I want to say, and I review my invention work. Then I just start writing, and I write everything I can think of that relates to my topic. It ends up being a glorified type of freewrite. I don't try to organize or censor as I work, I just dump the words out onto the page. Then I scratch out and punctuate and rearrange and add what's missing.

Every writer approaches the act of writing differently; whether you prefer to outline in detail or just jump right in, keep an open mind and be willing to make major changes to your piece. This type of writing project is a very young first draft—a newborn piece of magickal writing, one that will be revised many times before it's finished. For now, it exists to be manipulated and reshaped. Imagine you were going to make a new wand: you'd select and cut the wood, peel the bark, sand and seal it, decorate, carve, and finally bless and consecrate the new tool. Writing is much like that—it's a slow, steady process of creation, often with many steps.

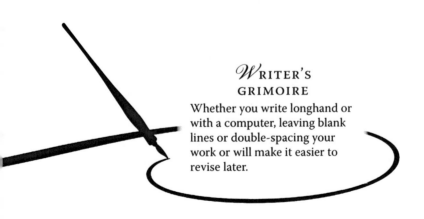

*W*RITER'S GRIMOIRE

Whether you write longhand or with a computer, leaving blank lines or double-spacing your work or will make it easier to revise later.

REVISING YOUR WORK

All good writing involves revision—and lots of it. This is true whether you're crafting a story or writing a ritual for your coven or circle. To revise a piece is to "re-vision" it, literally "to see it again" with fresh eyes. When you work with revision, you might add new content, move content around within the piece, take something out, or make changes at the sentence level. The critical point is that revision means *change*. When you revise your first draft, it becomes a second draft, and the second draft of your essay should look different from the first one. Good writers work through multiple revisions and multiple drafts of a project before considering it finished. (Actually, good writers never consider anything finished: they can always find something they'd like to tweak a little!)

There are four levels of revision: global, organizational (or local), sentence-level, and proofreading. Start at the top and work your way down the list.

Global Revision

When you have a raw first draft, you're ready to consider whether it needs a global revision—that is, a conceptual or "main idea" revision. Ask yourself these questions:

1. Does my paper/ritual/story have a guiding central idea or thesis? (Essays and nonfiction typically have a thesis or guiding central element, while works of fiction have a core idea.) Does the thesis or idea extend throughout the work? Have I veered off course at any point?

2. Is my topic big enough to be interesting, but not so big as to be unmanageable? Do I need to narrow or expand my topic or central idea?

3. Have I given enough information to make my points clear, to bring my characters to life, to create a vivid setting, etc.?

4. Are any parts confusing?

Work through these questions honestly, revising as extensively as you need to. Don't be afraid to do this—revision, remember, is a critical part of good writing. The more willing you are to see your work with clear eyes and to make changes, the better it will be. As part of your revision process, it may be helpful to ask someone to read your essay at this point—someone with fresh eyes can be helpful in answering the above questions.

Organizational Revision

Where global revision deals with conceptual issues affecting the entire piece, organizational revision aims to improve its structure and the logical order of its ideas. Most of this has to do with the structure and organization of paragraphs, so you might think of it as "paragraph level" revision. Work through this type of revision when you have a fully developed draft, or any time you make significant changes. Note that this applies to both nonfiction and fiction, in which it's important to arrange scenes (episodes of "action" between characters, setting, and natural events) and exposition (instances in which the narrator is explaining what is happening) in such a way that the reader can easily follow what's happening.

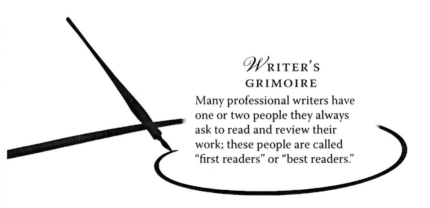

$\mathcal{W}$RITER'S GRIMOIRE

Many professional writers have one or two people they always ask to read and review their work; these people are called "first readers" or "best readers."

1. Does each paragraph start with a clear topic sentence and then focus on that idea?

2. Are the paragraphs in logical order?

3. Is there any place where I need to give more information?

4. Is there any redundancy?

If you feel like your work needs reorganization, here's a good trick: take a hard copy of the piece and cut it (with scissors) into its separate paragraphs. Then move the pieces around like a jigsaw puzzle, trying out different organizational patterns. Another suggestion is to ask your first reader to look through the paper again. If anything is unclear or out of order, she'll point it out.

Sentence-Level Revision

This is all about fine-tuning, about using language and words to make each sentence clear, yet rich and full of texture. Use sentence-level revision when you're well along with your writing project and ready to shine it up a little.

1. Read your draft aloud to hear the piece's "rhythm"—the way it flows from one idea to the next. Trust your ear: if anything sounds odd or clunky, it probably is.

2. Listen for too-long or too-short sentences. Although a mix of lengths is good, some long sentences may need to be divided in two, while short ones may need to be merged.

3. Listen for unintended changes in tense. Our spoken language tends to flip back and forth between past, present, and conditional tenses; when writing, it's important not to do this, as it can create confusion for the reader.

4. Look for places that could use images, alliteration, or other special effects (see Chapter 6).

Proofreading Your Work

This final step in the process of revision is all about catching and correcting errors and mistakes that will distract from the beauty of your work.

1. Read your draft aloud again and listen for errors in grammar. Consult your favorite writer's guide with questions (see the Resources section for recommendations).

2. Check your spelling. It's okay to begin with the computer spellchecker, but it's not foolproof: always proofread with your own eyes and your favorite dictionary, too. Look especially for misused homonyms, such as to/too and their/there/they're.

3. Check the punctuation. Again, a writer's guide can help.

And now . . . congratulations! That's a completed piece of writing you're holding on to!

 _____

1. Choose a simple prompt and use it to generate a brain-stormed list of ideas. Then use one of those items to create a cluster.

2. Using the brainstormed list from exercise 1, expand one or two items into a freewrite, then use the freewrite to carry out a looping exercise.

3. Using one of the ideas generated in exercise 1 or 2, expand it into a piece of writing—something simple, like a journal entry, a letter, or the description of a process, for example. Try to write at least one page.

4. For the next week, practice freewriting for at least ten minutes each day, with or without a prompt (see Chapter 14 for prompts).

four

JOURNAL KEEPING

Yesterday was a full moon, a total lunar eclipse, and a blood moon, all on one day. I watched the whole thing, start to finish. It was spectacular—started about 6:15 p.m. with a cookie-bite out of the moon, then finished after 11. The moon changed shades from a deep, rough pink to a brownish-red. Through the binoculars it was especially beautiful. I put my wands-in-progress and a chalice of water out to be charged under the moon. I also drew down the energy a little bit—it made me tremble. This has to be one of the most special sights I've ever seen. I'm ebullient, energized!

Most magickal folks keep a journal, or even two or three—notebooks or electronic files that combine pleasure and practicality, serving our need to capture our own thoughts and feelings as well as the concrete details of our lives. A good many magickal groups and solitaries likewise keep collective journals, grimoires, or extensive Books of Shadows summarizing their traditions, beliefs, practices, and initiatory policies.

Journals tend to be as varied as the people who write in them—yours might feature anything from the details of your last Sabbat to recollections of a magickal initiation to a sketch of the moon phases seen over a week of clear night skies. Regardless of content, each journal begins as a blank slate—a *tabula rasa*—for ideas, observations, insights, and personal reflections. It becomes a sort of mental camera, a place to capture snapshots of memory that can be recalled later and expanded into longer, creative works. Your general "writing journal" and your magickal journals are important to your *sub rosa* work—the words you write for your eyes only.

Historically, journals have also tracked explorations on a larger scale. Captain's logs and scientists' logbooks recorded details that would otherwise have been lost. Imagine what we might have missed if Paracelsus hadn't tracked his work in leechcraft and alchemy, or if Copernicus hadn't recorded his explorations of the night sky.

*M*AGICKAL MENTION

In medieval times, the Anglo-Saxon term *leech* was the English word for practitioners of all types of healing (a physician), while *leechcraft* referred to the art of healing or herbology. Alchemy is a medieval forerunner of chemistry, based on the supposed transformation of matter. It was concerned particularly with attempts to convert base metals into gold or to find a universal elixir of life. Classical alchemy is heavily allegorical, often referring to the transformation of the human soul.

In the same way, over time, journaling can help you track your magickal and spiritual progress. Your growth as a writer—and as a magickal writer—takes you along a unique path, and journaling can trace and shadow your developing skill. Let's summarize these benefits.

A journal helps you become a more creative, inspired writer. Use your journal as a place to work on this book's Scribbulus exercises, revise and polish your pieces, or jot down ideas or invention work. All your journals are private—no one need see them but you, so feel free to take risks. And since practice makes perfect, the more you add to your journal, the better. Reviewing your progress over the weeks and months will reveal your developing skills.

A journal functions as a filing cabinet for ideas. Use it to capture thoughts, to freewrite, and otherwise store short pieces that may later blossom into something stunning. Write down ideas as they occur to you—don't trust them to memory! Set down the details of a lunar eclipse, a bonfire, a garden come to fruition, a thunderstorm, or a powerful ritual.

A journal relieves stress. Turn to your journal when you're feeling tense or uncertain. Writing down your thoughts and feelings will help you feel lighter and can lead to surprising insights; future projects will be born of those lightbulb moments of personal revelation.

A journal increases your output. Sure, writing is fun, but it also takes discipline. The person who turns to a journal every day is developing a habit, one that makes it easier to write and to keep writing regularly.

A journal links you to people and groups whose training and practices involve journals and other recordkeeping. The writing you do now may forge an important link in your spiritual or writing future. If you choose to undergo certain types of magickal training or apprenticeship, journaling will almost certainly play a role in your studies.

A journal is an excellent way to track personal transformation over time. With dedicated journal use, you'll be able to look back and map your journey, revisiting your discoveries, successes, and even the occasional snafu. You'll have objective proof of your developing skills, which will encourage you to push further.

And finally, thumbing through a beloved journal can be like sinking into a comfortable chair for **a long visit with an old friend.**

SPECIALIZED OR THEMATIC JOURNALS

In addition to a standard "writing journal," you may want to keep one or more specialized notebooks for specific kinds of magickal practice. For example:

- *Dream journal*: Record details of dreams, then reflect back on them later. For best results, keep the journal at your bedside and write in it immediately upon awakening. Dreams can be an important source of insight for memoir and fodder for short stories as well.

- *Divination journal*: For any divination work, record the date, time, outcomes, and effectiveness. Add sketches to recall specific layouts of cards, runes, and so on. Use reflection to fine-tune your future efforts.

- *Healing journal*: Every healer must keep careful records, not only of her healing recipes and methods, but also of how each subject responded to the ministrations. Use a healing journal to record details of healing works, notes on your own studies, observations, and so on.

- *Herbal journal*: Record details of herbal workings, including recipes, processes, and results. Use sketches and maps to show the layout of a garden or a map of a wilderness site. Include descriptions of wildcrafting trips, where you gather herbs in the wilderness (using ethical practices, of course).

- *Nature journal*: In this, the nature writer's greatest tool, write about your outdoor travels, observations, and discoveries. Record the sense of wonder when watching a butterfly hatch from a cocoon, or seeing Earth's shadow settle across the moon in a lunar eclipse.

USING YOUR "WRITING JOURNAL"

If you've been working sequentially through this book, you already have a writing routine underway. Now it's time to bring your journal into that routine.

Start by setting aside time for journaling. Some people like to journal in the evening so they can reflect on the day. Others prefer early morning, when they feel freshest and can consider the day's as-yet unrealized possibilities. Create an environment that supports your creativity. Ignore e-mail, turn the cell phone off, kill the television—"unplug" from mundania and give yourself a chance to engage your innermost magickal self.

Begin every journaling session with a freewrite or some other kind of invention. Use your journal to explore ideas or to draft actual pieces of writing, and turn to it throughout the day whenever an idea needs to be captured and filed away for safekeeping. Set up separate pages for spell ideas, story titles, and so on. Take time every so often to flip back through your entries; use a highlighter to spotlight ideas or bits of strong or engaging writing that beg for further development or reflection. Your journal is the ideal place to record reactions to books, films, newspaper articles, discussions about magickal topics, etc. The idea you write down today might become fruitful tomorrow. Don't worry about your journal entries looking perfect. Remember, this is *sub rosa*: private.

Keep your journal (or at least a small pocket journal) with you all the time—be ready for anything that sparks a writing idea. Date each journal entry. Include the time, weather, moon phase, zodiacal sign, your location, or any other details that might be useful in the future. Over time, you may identify times, locations, lunar phases, or other correspondences that impact your writing.

Using the Process of Reflection in Your Journaling

The word *reflect* comes from a Latin verb that means "to bend back." Magick practitioners often use reflection, looking back on spells and rituals to decide what worked and what might need tweaking. Writing is no different, and reflection is a great way to work with ideas.

How to do a written reflection

1. When you experience a moment of intense observation or emotional response, pull out your journal and use the experience to craft a freewrite. Include as many sensory details as possible, e.g., sight, sound, smell, taste, and touch. It's fine to write a journal entry explaining how a rainstorm looked; it's even better if you can tell how the rain felt, or what kind of sound it made, or how it smelled. These details will kindle your memory later on and make the reflecting process easier.

*M*AGICKAL
MENTION

In magickal practice, "correspondences" refer to shared qualities or associations between materials. For example, the magickal element of earth corresponds with the direction north, mountains, the color green, the suit of pentacles in the tarot, the season of winter, and the zodiacal signs of Capricorn, Taurus, and Virgo.

2. When done, set your notes aside, and don't look at them again for at least a few days—longer, if possible. No peeking!

3. At a later time, review the notes and reflect, allowing the images and memories to resurface. Expand your notes, adding more details, or even do a second freewrite.

4. You might then use the notes to craft a story, charm, ritual, or other work.

> *Sept. 2004; Yosemite National Park. At sunset, cloud shadows swept over El Capitan and the sky changed to that beautiful blue of deep dusk, trees standing out like black crystal against the night sky. The fading sun was replaced by a brilliant full moon, the light making the granite cliffs seem to glow as if from huge light bulbs deep within. By the time we returned to our camp at 8,000 feet, the moonlight was so bright we could read without flashlights or lanterns. We sat by the campfire, wrapped in scratchy wool blankets and sipping mugs of cocoa spiked with peppermint schnapps. The sharp, cold air, the smell and crackling warmth of the fire, the rich, minted cocoa, the peaceful comfort of the remote setting, the sound of coyotes barking nearby, and the glow of the moon made it an incredible evening.*

The vignette above is taken from notes I made during a camping trip at Yosemite National Park. When I read those notes now and think about that vacation, the sensory details of crackling fire and hot cocoa and moonlight and mint and wood smoke and barking coyotes bring it back with great clarity. I could easily expand these notes into something else . . . a poem, perhaps.

Sunset shadows sweeping
granite cliffs and
dark sky.
Then, Moonrise.
We sipped cocoa and
drifted into a night of
hot fire,
cold air,
and coyote song.

I could just as easily write a short memoir piece about the trip, and how those majestic surroundings affect me. Or I might use the images of light, dark, and movement in my next nighttime ritual. However you use it, reflection is a powerful tool for writers and magickal practitioners, for we never know which memories and observations will end up taking on special meaning. Make lots of image-rich entries in your journal, and develop a regular habit of reading and reflecting on those notes. You'll reap the benefits.

PROTECTING YOUR JOURNALS

Most of us believe that we shouldn't pick up or look into another person's personal journal, for to do so diminishes its power. A journal is a tool, and magickal tools shouldn't be handled without the owner's permission; at the very least, no one should read your writings without your okay.

When you aren't using your writing journal, keep it in a safe place, away from curious or prying eyes. Write a note on the first page informing people that the contents are private. You might even shield or cloak your journal (see Chapter 17). A simple way to discourage unwelcome eyes is to tie it closed with a length of ribbon—perhaps black (for banishing), blue (for general protection), or patterned with symbols. Color aside, a snug ribbon tied around your journal will make it impossible for anyone to open it accidentally, and will slow down anyone trying to open it on purpose. Tie the ends of the ribbon in a square knot; this is perfect in a magickal sense, as its shape reflects balance and its physical nature is security incarnate.

You may wish to create a ritual or blessing to consecrate or dedicate your journal, asking that it become a tool of wisdom, guidance, and focus. Here's a simple blessing that could be inscribed inside the journal's front cover.

Guard my words,
Keep them safe
Here within
This treasured place.

Sign with magickal name, date, and perhaps a sigil or bindrune. For extra oomph, write the blessing with a magickal alphabet and/or colored ink—perhaps blue (for protection) or silver-gray (for knowledge and wisdom).

*M*AGICKAL
MENTION

A bindrune is created by combining two or more runic letters to form a unique sigil or inscription. See Chapter 12 for more about working with sigils, and the appendix for the runic alphabet.

Scribbulus _____

1. Use the instructions in this chapter to practice a reflection. You might choose a fresh, compelling moment to write about, e.g., a rainstorm, a place of great natural beauty, a moving magickal experience. Or, you might focus on a simpler moment: a family meal, time spent working on a new wand, ruminations on a long walk with your dog, etc. Responding to "everyday" moments can be especially illuminating, as this helps us appreciate the magick that's part of our everyday lives.

2. During a nature outing, find a comfortable spot and spend thirty minutes being as quiet and motionless as you can. Use your senses to perceive what happens around you. After thirty minutes, thank the beings and energies of the surrounding area for allowing you to share in their presence. Leave the space quietly, leaving no trace. Make a journal entry about your observations and feelings. Describe any magickal properties or presences that you were aware of.

3. Take a magickal journey—on paper. Imagine a place you've always wanted to go. Create a journal entry that describes the experience. What does the place look, smell, and sound like? How do you respond? What surprises you?

five

ꙄEEING AND ꙄEMEMBERING

One of the best ways to work with writing is through the process of observation—the use of careful attention to notice or record things happening around you. At its heart, good observation takes time and practice, for observation doesn't come naturally to most of us: in our busy everyday lives, we tend to focus on whatever we're concerned with at the moment—within our own personal sphere—and we often fail to see or appreciate what's happening around us. This is true in the magick world as well: how many of us have been so focused on a magickal working that we fail to notice the surprising result or implication that occurs outside of our expectations?

Writers *must* be consummate observers, and the skills of observation can be practiced and polished. A good way to practice noticing more is to settle yourself in an interesting public location and wait to see and hear what happens around you. You might begin with a coffee shop, a city street, or a local park. As the people and animals around you become accustomed to your presence, you'll fade into the place's background—more or less vanishing—and you'll begin to see and perceive details you would have missed before.

As you observe, take careful notes, using sensory details to help you recall the scene later. What do you hear? See? Smell? What time of day is it? What's the weather like? What is the lunar phase? How do you feel while watching the world pass by? Are you able to pick up on energies around you?

A single instance of observation allows you to capture specific, one-time details. If you want to study repeated patterns and cycles, you'll need to observe the same setting over and over again. This is important if you're trying to capture the impact or effects of seasonal changes, cyclical events, the duration of magickal practices, the over-time outcome of divination readings, or similar long-running/repeated occurrences. As you hone your skills of perception, you'll start to appreciate the cyclical, ever-shifting balance that's all around you. You'll see the magickal and material worlds with renewed curiosity and understanding, your new-honed awareness buoying your writing and supporting your magickal studies. Becoming a better observer will also help you become a better writer; given time, you'll surprise yourself as observations naturally begin to take form in your mind's eye, shapeshifting into written compositions.

CLOAKING AND SHIELDING

The best observers fade or slip into the background, creating a "blind" from which to observe while remaining more or less hidden from others. You can enhance this observer invisibility with intentional shielding and cloaking. Shielding is the practice of creating a protective energy layer around oneself, offering protection from magickal effects as well as environmental overload, including noises and negative energies. When we create shields, we "harden" our auric fields into psychic fields, and protect ourselves against unwanted psychic energy.

Cloaking is similar to shielding but implies "draping" yourself with an energy field that absorbs energy and makes you inconspicuous, or at least harder to "see." Whereas you might visualize a shield as a hard shell that energy bounces off of, think of a cloak as a soft, black woolen blanket, which not only hides you but also absorbs light and sound. If you're well cloaked, people will be unaware of your presence and will not recall having seen you, even though they may have passed very close by.

For details on practicing cloaking and shielding, refer to a standard magickal text (see Resources). You'll also find a little more about shielding in Chapter 17.

THE SYNESTHETE

True synesthesia is a neurological (brain-based) condition in which two or more of the body's sensory systems are abnormally linked. When a person with synesthesia (a synesthete) hears a sound, they might simultaneously "see" a color. Or, they might stroke a textured surface and suddenly perceive a taste in their mouth. Some kind of synesthesia—of varying intensity—occurs in up to 4 percent of humans and the tendency is strongly hereditary. Modern imaging has

*M*AGICKAL
MENTION

Each of us has an aura—a biomagnetic energy field that issues from us and from all living things. We can manipulate our own auras to create various magickal effects. Many people can also see auras emanating from themselves and others.

shown specific brain responses during these events and psychological research has also documented measurable behavioral changes in synesthetic individuals.

Because of their sensory "overlay," synesthetes respond uniquely to what's around them, and they may be strikingly successful as poets, artists, writers, and musicians. They also tend to have a superior memory. However, they're also unusually sensitive to sensory stimuli and may experience left/right confusion and difficulties with logical processes, such as math.

In magickal terms, synesthetes are good at seeing auras and energy, particularly around the heads of their loved ones. They're also good at certain divination activities, including scrying, mirror writing, and clairaudience.

If you've been gifted with synesthesia, rejoice in the special access this gives you to experiencing and interpreting multisensory stimuli. If you're like most people and your five senses speak to each other in the usual ways, you can still embrace synesthesia as a writing tool. Think about the senses creatively, e.g., asking yourself how a waterfall would taste, the color of the words in a spoken charm, the sound made by the act of grounding, etc. These kinds of creative imaginings can lead you to fresh ideas and even to new awareness. Use your writing notebook to record your sensory workings, and make sure to reflect on the process (see Chapter 4).

*M*AGICKAL
MENTION

Clairaudience is the ability to hear or perceive sounds that aren't within the normal hearing range. It may also indicate sensitivity to "inner" voices and vibrations.

WORKING WITH MEMORY

It's clear that memory—through its ability to spark personal insight and discovery—is a critical aspect of personal narrative. In some ways, memory is more real than the here and now, because we regard memory with a perspective of permanence that locates it as a set moment in time, transcending past and present and making us the narrators of our own life stories. But memory can also be spurious. When we can't remember something, it might be a matter of organic failure: something physical (fatigue, stress, etc.) is preventing us from accessing a specific memory. Or it may be selective: for some reason, we *choose* not to remember. The distinction is important, because refusal to remember—even if unintentional—is an indication of an emotion begging to be explored.

Since memories are so important to personal narratives, you may wish to enhance your recall ability. There are many ways, both magickal and mundane, to improve and support memory and in turn improve your writing.

Mundane Approaches

First of all, eat well. A diet of organic, unprocessed, highly colored foods (e.g., sweet potatoes, broccoli, purple grapes, blueberries, etc.) is loaded with antioxidants and has a positive effect on memory. Blueberries are an especially profound memory food. Take a

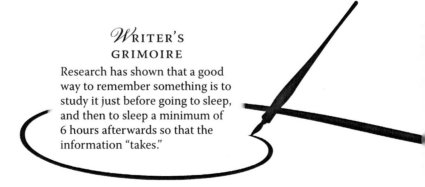

Writer's
GRIMOIRE
Research has shown that a good way to remember something is to study it just before going to sleep, and then to sleep a minimum of 6 hours afterwards so that the information "takes."

multivitamin and Omega-3 supplements; both have been linked to improved memory. Drink lots of water every day: your body needs two quarts of water each day for optimal metabolic functions, including memory. Be sure to get enough sleep as well. Respect your own body's rhythms. If you're a morning person, your memory is sharpest in the morning and fades in the evening. Give yourself time to think: processing and reflecting are important parts of being a writer and require time and energy. Challenge your brain every day by reading and studying new things. Research suggests a "use it or lose it" relationship between aging and memory.

Magickal Approaches

Grounding and centering before a memory session can help you slip into a state that boosts awareness and recall. Meditation may actually help access memory. Honeysuckle, lilac, and rosemary are known to stimulate mental powers, and some people may find their memory improved by either a mild stimulant (e.g., caffeine) or a relaxing herbal tea (chamomile is ideal for this). Jasmine, myrrh, and nutmeg support meditation, as do the endorphin-stimulating agents in dark chocolate. Herbal sachets, scented candles, and oil diffusers can bring these helpful essences into your writing space.

Don't underestimate the power of a good memory charm. A brief ritual or spell in which you speak aloud and materialize your intention to remember will support your efforts, especially if it's surrounded by the right correspondences (see Chapter 16).

UH-OH . . . IT'S WRITER'S BLOCK . . .

We all know what that means. You sit, staring at the empty page, and haven't a clue as to where to begin. Writer's block strikes everyone from time to time. If you fall victim, try one of the following:

- Spend 10–15 minutes freewriting.

- Go for a walk. Quit thinking about the writing project and instead tune in to your surroundings.

- Do something artistic or creative; draw, work with clay, make a collage, or work on illuminating your work (see Chapter 13).

- Write a letter by hand.

- Pick up your writer's notebook and go through it. Enjoy yourself. If an idea surfaces, so much the better.

- Read, curled up with a favorite book and a cup of tea.

- Take a thirty-minute nap.

- Work some magick. Burn herbs for inspiration, or sip an herbal brew designed to invoke creativity—try mint with a pinch of clove (see Chapter 16).

- Put your writing task away and come back to it tomorrow.

- Call upon your muse . . .

Invoking the Muse

Poets and writers have long sought the divine inspiration of the gods. To muse over a piece of writing is to spend time absorbed in its creation. (Writers do a lot of musing!) In ancient Greece, the nine muses were goddess-daughters of Zeus—king of the gods— and the goddess Mnemosyne, the goddess of memory. Each muse was linked to one of the traditional arts and sciences:

Calliope, muse of rhetoric and epic poetry, is usually shown holding a rolled scroll.

Clio, muse of history, is depicted reading from a scroll.

Erato, muse of marriage and love poetry, plays a lyre.

Euterpe, muse of music and lyric poetry, plays two flutes (at once).

Melpomene, muse of tragedy, holds a "sad face" dramatic mask, the club of Hercules, and a wreath of grape leaves.

Polyhymnia, muse of sacred hymn, is shown singing.

Terpsichore, muse of dance and dance music, dances with a tambourine.

Thalia, muse of comedy and idyllic poetry, counters Melpomene. Thalia holds a "happy face" dramatic mask, a shepherd's crook, and a wreath of ivy leaves.

Urania, muse of astronomy and the heavens, holds a globe of Earth and a wand.

The ancient Greeks believed that poetry, music, and other arts were gifts of the gods, and before any act of artistic performance or creation, they would invoke the gods and the appropriate muse, seeking inspiration. Homer's *Odyssey* begins with the words, "Tell me, O Muse, of that ingenious hero who traveled far and wide. . . ." * Ancient and modern bards and many poets continue this practice.

You, too, can call upon the muse, whether it's one of the classic nine sisters (above) or your own personal version. The muse is something different for each of us. Once you've discovered your own, invite her (or him) to join you at your writing desk. Find out what kind of magick she gravitates to. Light some candles, diffuse a little oil, set out stones, or wrap yourself in magickal garb. (The muses are said to be fond of hazelnuts and the color purple.) Let your mind open to inspiration and welcome her in.

How will you know when your muse finds you? If you sit down to write and the words pour forth, composing a beautiful little charm

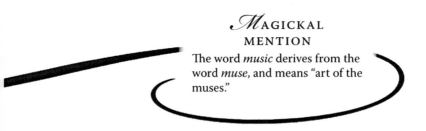

MAGICKAL MENTION

The word *music* derives from the word *muse*, and means "art of the muses."

---

*Homer. *The Odyssey*. Maynard Mack, ed. *The Norton Anthology of World Masterpieces (Expanded Edition)*. New York: Norton, 1997.

without much thought, and if, when you look at the clock, you realize that three hours have gone by without your notice, well, my friend, your muse has paid a visit.

Just for fun . . . Mnemosyne's name comes from a Greek root meaning "mindful," and from her name comes our modern word, *mnemonic*. A mnemonic is a device inspiring mindfulness—a pattern of letters, ideas, or associations that boosts memory and assists in remembering something. For example, here's a famous poem for remembering the order of the zodiacal constellations:

> *The Ram, the Bull, the Heavenly Twins,*
> *And next the Crab, the Lion shines,*
> *The Virgin and the Scales.*
> *The Scorpion, Archer, and the Goat,*
> *The Man who holds the Watering Pot,*
> *And Fish with glittering scales.*

Experiment with using mnemonic devices to help you remember details for later reflection and writing.

Wherever You Find Muses, There Are Also Sirens

No, not the rescue-vehicle type—I'm talking about the sirens that lurk on rocks, inviting you toward shore only to break your boat of ambitions into kindling. In Greek mythology, the sirens were women

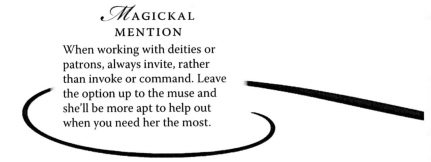

*M*AGICKAL
MENTION
When working with deities or patrons, always invite, rather than invoke or command. Leave the option up to the muse and she'll be more apt to help out when you need her the most.

or winged creatures whose singing attracted unwary sailors, causing them to steer their boats toward the coastal rocks and a quick demise. While on his journeys, Homer's Odysseus famously lashed himself to his own mainmast in order to be certain he could resist the sirens' attractions.

In modern times, the word *siren* has come to mean anything that's alluring or fascinating but also dangerous in some way. To a writer who's trying to work, the outside world is full of the sirens' songs—only instead of beautiful women, these sirens look like televisions, cell phones, and e-mail accounts. As with everything in the universe, one thing balances another. Respect the gift of the muses and call upon them as needed, but fear the call of the sirens and don't be afraid to lash yourself to your own mainmast: turn off the TV, kill the phone, and limit e-mail time to half an hour once or twice a day. Give yourself time and space to settle into your writing undistracted. May your sails billow and your path be true over calm seas.

 *Scribbulus* _____

1. Dedicate a fresh page in your writing notebook to writer's block. Title it "What To Do When I Have Writer's Block." Make a list of approaches that work for you.

2. The next time you engage in a magickal working, give extra attention to observation. Open your senses and intuition to not only the physical nature of the working, but to the metaphysical and spiritual as well. What are you aware of? What forces do you feel at work? What did you learn? Record your findings in your journal; wait a few days, then reflect on what you wrote.

3. Consider your own muse. Who might he or she be? Free-write on this idea, opening yourself to discovery. How might you invite the muse into your writing space? Develop a simple ritual to invite and welcome your muse, or write an invocation or "musing" to use at the start of each writing session.

six

Your Words, Transformed

Imagine having the chance to write in a magickal room that is humming with energy and alive with colors, scents, and textures. Imagine that vivid fabrics adorn a group of easy chairs while a central table is spread with a brilliant-green cloth patterned in Celtic knotwork. Set around the room are multicolored candles, diffusers of essential oils, and half a dozen glass bowls, each brimming with scented dried herbs. Shimmering stones and crystals are scattered on the tablecloth among heaps of colored pencils, inks, and textured papers. A small fountain burbles on a corner table, and soft Native American flute music lingers in the background as flickering candlelight plays over the walls.

Just imagine writing in this setting, all your senses alive and tingling. You, the reader, probably have a pretty good image in your head now, complete with the sensory details described above.

Description and figurative writing allows a writer to invoke the five senses and invite them into her work, creating texture, sound, color, scent, and light on the page. Good description is an important part of all writing, and in magickal writing, it's a vital element of craft. Even more important, using it is lots of fun.

Multisensory Imagery

Multisensory images are those that place the five senses—sight, sound, touch, taste, and smell—into your writing, evoking a strong response in the reader. Sensory details bring your characters and settings to life, so that your readers can *see* them in their mind's eye.

Let's look at this excerpt from a nature journal:

> *Here, the river runs wide and flat. I imagine my arms and legs are the veins of the maple leaf, and I feel my body as light as the leaf's papery skin. Somewhere inside myself, there is ancient familiarity and longing, not just remnant from memories of splashing on the shores of Eagle Creek or the Sandy River, of the Columbia or the Clackamas or the Willamette, but lingering from an ageless part of me that remembers days when the bond was strong, in a time long ago. It smolders in the part of me that finds a memory in the*

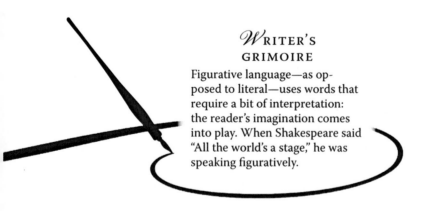

𝒲RITER'S GRIMOIRE

Figurative language—as opposed to literal—uses words that require a bit of interpretation: the reader's imagination comes into play. When Shakespeare said "All the world's a stage," he was speaking figuratively.

*smell of burning cedar, in the sound of a fish breaking the surface
or a dry branch snapping underneath my feet.**

This passage—rich with sensory imagery—is dense and complicated and plucks at the reader's poetic heartstrings. Look at this sentence, which uses scent, sound, sight, and texture to great effect:

*It smolders in the part of me that finds a memory in the smell of
burning cedar, in the sound of a fish breaking the surface or a dry
branch snapping underneath my feet.*

Can you almost smell the cedar? Hear the splash of a fish or the crack of the branch? That's the power of imagery at work. Effective sensory description means using enough details, but not overdoing it. Tricky? Indeed. Use too little description and your writing will feel uncertain and confused; use too much, and it'll be weighed down by heavy details. Good description gives enough information to set an image, but leaves enough *unsaid* that the readers can envision a full picture for themselves. This pulls the reader into the writing and helps them engage with the world that has been created on the page. In magickal writing—a guided meditation, or a ritual, perhaps—good description adds to the participant's experience.

Ways of Comparison

Writers often find themselves making comparisons in their writing, and the most common ways to do this are with simile or metaphor. A simile is a written, abstract comparison that uses *like* or *as*. The comparison is explicit: straightforward and obvious.

"I feel my body as light as the leaf's papery skin."

---

*Pesznecker, Katie. "River Reflections." *Honoring Our River: 2000. A Student
Anthology Collected from Throughout the Willamette River Watershed.* Eds. John
Femal, Steve Jones, Kathleen Dean Moore, et al. Eugene, OR: Eugene Water and
Electric Board, the Willamette Restoration Initiative and Wildwood/Mahonia,
2000.

A metaphor is a comparison made without using *like* or *as*. In a metaphor, the comparison may be partly concealed, or just hinted at. With simile, the comparison is apparent, but with metaphor, the reader must dig a little to get at the underlying meaning. From the above piece:

> "I imagine my arms and legs are the veins of the maple leaf."

Personification

In personification, an animal, inanimate object, or even an abstract term is given lifelike or human characteristics. Personification helps you create drama by making the non-human seem alive or subject to human problems or the human condition. This is a common trick in magickal or fantasy writing, as when a sword or magick wand comes to life, or when a magickal force or creature speaks with a human voice. Personification crops up in mundane life when we describe objects, such as our cars, as having thoughts and feelings:

> The old Ford is tired.

Alliteration, Assonance, and Onomatopoeia

Alliteration and assonance use the sounds within words to create emphasis, cadence, or rhythm in prose or poetry. These devices are especially useful in spells, rituals, and chants; the sound techniques help create rhythm in the words, and the rhythm echoes the ritual structure.

Alliteration is a repeated consonant sound at the beginning of nearby words in a line of text. Alliteration can also be internal, in which case the repeated sound falls on stressed syllables rather than always striking the first letter of selected words. Internal alliteration is also called consonance.

> "Here, the <u>r</u>iver <u>r</u>uns . . ."
> "I feel my body as <u>l</u>ight as the <u>l</u>eaf's papery skin."

Assonance is the occurrence of the same vowel or vowel sound at the beginning of or within adjacent or connected words. Assonance uses repeated sounds to gain the reader's attention.

> "I imagine my arms and legs are the v<u>ei</u>ns of the m<u>a</u>ple leaf . . ."
>
> "D<u>ou</u>ble, d<u>ou</u>ble, toil and tr<u>ou</u>ble."

In the first example, a 'long-a' sound is emphasized repeatedly. In the second example, from Shakespeare, the 'uh' vowel is repeated, as well as the internal 'b' sounds (consonance). Alliteration and assonance were particular favorites of medieval poets and chanters, with the stressed syllables and similar sounds adding to the cadence of the piece and creating a strong rhythmic feeling.

Another word-sound device, onomatopoeia (pronounced AH-nuh-MAH-tuh-PEE-uh), refers to a word that sounds like what it's describing. Though these words vary among languages, they can provide a fun sound to go along with the meaning you wish to convey. The words *sizzle, thunk, clip-clop,* and *cuckoo* are examples of onomatopoeia.

Parallelism and Repetition

In parallelism, words, phrases, clauses, etc., are arranged in a way that creates a side-by-side repetition. Parallelism is a way of organizing ideas structurally; it also creates rhythmicity in prose, poetry, and chants. Notice the parallel structure of "in the" below:

> "It smolders <u>in the part of me</u> that finds a memory <u>in the smell</u> of burning cedar, <u>in the sound</u> of a fish breaking the surface . . ."

Repetition is similar to parallelism; it uses repeated elements but doesn't require a parallel structure. Repetition adds a sense of rhythm and creates continuity, as in the repeated names of bodies of water, below:

". . . not just remnants from memories of splashing on the shores of <u>Eagle Creek</u> or the <u>Sandy River</u>, of the <u>Columbia</u> or the <u>Clacka-mas</u> or the <u>Willamette</u>, but lingering from an ageless part of me . . ."

Simplicity

Aim for simplicity in your writing. That's not to say you should avoid using figurative language, just make sure that every word you use is doing work in the sentence. Otherwise, keep your writing clear and uncluttered.

Too wordy:

> She put on a cloak of soft, purple, evanescent, crushed, touch-able velvet, that swirled around her thin legs like a prowling black cat when she swept noiselessly through the empty, dark-ened, cavernous room.

Better:

> She donned a cloak of purple velvet that swirled around her as she swept though the darkened room.

What sounds like wordiness is sometimes created by too many short sentences.

Wordy:

> The Wizard kept a stave with him at all times. He had had the stave for twenty years. He considered the stave to be like a friend.

Better:

> Having owned his stave for twenty years and considering it a friend, the Wizard kept it close.

There are a few words and phrases that should be avoided in writing—they're rarely necessary and will weaken your prose 99 percent of the time. Such weak words and phrases include:

- a little, a lot

- as a matter of fact, in light of the fact

- basically, virtually, essentially

- in a real sense

- kind of, sort of

- much, some, many, very

- What I am trying to say is . . .

The easiest way to judge a word or phrase's worthiness is to read the sentence with and without it. Which way is better? Which sounds stronger? Which is clearer? Trust your ear and choose carefully, for each word must do enough work to earn its keep; if it's just lying around on the couch, eating potato chips and watching TV, get rid of it. This rule is true in writing and it's especially true in ritual and spellwork, where words come alive with magick and intention. Each word must carry its weight.

PUTTING IT ALL TOGETHER

Imagine the above techniques as a set of runes: while they're stored in the same bag, each one looks a little different and has its own specific powers and abilities. When you study runes, you learn to respect each one for its unique attributes. The same is true of descriptive writing techniques, and by learning and practicing their magick, you'll add a useful set of tools to your writer's kit.

Scribbulus _____

1. Go for a walk and pick up a rock. Write a short descriptive piece about the rock, using as many of the techniques described in this chapter as possible. See if you can paint a verbal image without using the words *stone, rock, pebble, crystal, gravel,* or *gem.*

2. Take a journal entry—or any other short piece of writing—and work in a few words that use alliteration. How does this change the sound, rhythm, or tone of the piece?

3. Play with personification. Write a short piece in which you imagine that your favorite magickal or writing tool has come to life and is offering its thoughts or opinions.

seven

TELLING STORIES

o you love stories, both hearing them and telling them? Do you fancy yourself a storyteller? Would you like to try writing down your own stories? If you've answered yes to any of these questions, this chapter is for you. In this chapter we're going to talk about the spectrum of storytelling.

The word *story* comes from a Latin word meaning "history," and long before humans began to write, we told stories through speech, song, gesture, and dance. Storytelling became a way for people to record histories and accumulated knowledge and traditions. Many cultures had their own lorekeepers; for instance, the African *griot* (GREE-oh) was a learned tribesman who sustained the tribe's knowledge of medicine (power), healing, and history. Chosen in boyhood, the griot-to-be spent his life memorizing generations of genealogy and lore and could sing or recite those records upon request, supporting the tribe's heritage and traditions. Ancient Scandinavian *skalds* composed and recited epic poems in honor of heroes and their heroic deeds. Magickal history had its bards, trained Druids who used music and story to preserve the history and lore of the Celtic people. Secret societies such as the Knights Templar and the Freemasons have maintained an unwritten sub rosa tradition over hundreds of years. Today's Druid groves, Wiccan covens, Wizards, and solitary magickal practitioners both foster and add to written collections of arcane knowledge, while still passing on traditions orally and via hands-on practice. Storytelling remains one of the oldest of the bardic arts. Attend a Pagan or Druid gathering and a bardic circle—complete with stories, ballads, and drinking horn—is guaranteed to be a key part of the event.

To tell a story is to craft a narrative. The word *narrative* means "to relate or tell," and a narrative is a spoken or written account of connected events—otherwise known as a story. Each of us already has all the tools needed to tell stories: experiences, memories, and thoughts. Through experiences we build memories, and our memories are then shaped by new experiences. It's a never-ending, swirling cycle of magick, a chicken-and-egg situation where one can lose track of which is more powerful: the original experience or the shapeshifting imagination that results.

THE SPOKEN NARRATIVE

A spoken narrative is yet another term for a story, and a storyteller is the one who tells the tale. The word *tell* comes from roots that mean "tale," and storytellers are known as tale-tellers and also as raconteurs, fabulists, jongleurs, and anecdotalists. Records of storytelling are found in virtually every culture and in many languages, including Sanskrit, Old German, Latin, Chinese, Greek, Icelandic, and Old Slavonic. Storytellers see story as a traditional, oral narrative that uses style, characters, physical presence, and shared experience to pass on accumulated wisdom, beliefs, and values. Simply put, storytellers use tales to teach and entertain. A "storytelling" is a live, in-person presentation of a story to an audience, with direct contact between teller and listener. The *live* requirement is important—a story read from a book or heard from radio or television doesn't qualify as storytelling in the traditional sense. The in-person storyteller uses language, vocalization, gestures, and presence to communicate the story to the listeners; each listener soaks up the performance and "sees" the story in his or her mind. The listener's past experiences, beliefs, education, and culture play a big role in how the story is interpreted. Because of this, each story takes its own shape in the mind of the listener and becomes something unique and important.

Why should magick practitioners be interested in storytelling? Most of us are consummate fabulists. We tell stories to entertain, teach, and impart wisdom, sharing tales that display ethical behavior and the consequences of decision making. Humans have probably told tales from the moment they learned to speak, and our stories have always served many purposes. Stories provide a way of accounting for the physical world, allowing people to explain the land, seasons, and substance of their very lives. Storytelling serves an important social activity; humans are communal beings, and have an intrinsic need to share their experiences. In Stone Age times, storytelling filled many a dark evening, with the tellers reenacting hunts or other thrilling events.

Stories have always served a role in teaching, both in terms of moral codes and accepted behaviors. Through stories, children learned the legends of their own people and were shown models of adult behavior. They also had their behavior modified through stories of admonition or warning, e.g., the Boogey Man. Mythic tales held spiritual relevance and helped people appeal to or deal with spirits, gods, spirituality, and prophecy, while allegories provided examples of conduct. Even today, spiritual leaders—through sermons, counseling, and the bearing of tradition—are regarded as storytellers. Through stories, the actions and nature of one's ancestors could be recorded for posterity, helping the teller connect with their ancestors and conferring a kind of implied immortality. Tales become both art and craft, fulfilling an aesthetic need for beauty and providing a way to express creativity through language.

For magickal folks, storytelling may best be exemplified by the bard. The term has a Celtic origin, with a bard being one type of highly trained Druid. Most bards were also poets, reciting epics associated with cultural tradition and lineage. The word *bard* comes from the French *barde,* meaning "armor for the breast and flanks of a warhorse," which was based on the Arabic *bar d a'a,* meaning a saddlecloth or padded saddle. The bard was obviously well prepared for a challenging journey, and the bardic storyteller was in fact a traveling poet and musician—sort of a journeyman fabulist.

Bardic traditions are responsible for gathering and preserving many of our best epic tales, including:

- the Sumerian epic of Gilgamesh (and his friendship with Enkidu, the half-beast, half-man created to destroy him)

- the Iliad (Greek epic story of the Trojan War)

- the Odyssey (Greek epic story of Odysseus on his homeward journey from Troy)

- the Norse story of Sigurd (Siegfried) (including the Volsunga Saga, with the killing of a dragon Fafnir)

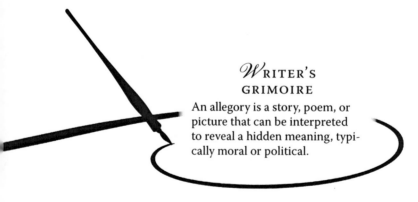

*W*RITER'S GRIMOIRE

An allegory is a story, poem, or picture that can be interpreted to reveal a hidden meaning, typically moral or political.

- the Merry Adventures of Robin Hood (an Englishman who, with his band of Merry Men, fought oppression)

- the Song of Roland (French; legendary tales of the knight)

- Sundiata, the epic of the Lion King (African; Sundiata overcomes handicaps to become King of Mali)

- the Tain (Irish; tale of the legendary hero Cuchulain)

- the Celtic Mabinogion

- the Ramayana (India)

And of course, those were eventually preserved in written form, which takes us to . . .

THE WRITTEN NARRATIVE

It's likely that the first story was penned not long after humans first learned to write, and it's thanks to writing that many of the oldest oral traditional narratives have been retained. One of the earliest records of storytelling is in the Egyptian Westcar Papyrus, in which the sons of the pyramid builder Cheops entertained their father with stories. The epic of Gilgamesh, which relates the story of a Sumerian king, is often cited as the world's oldest surviving story.

Written narratives can be based on truth, in which case we call them nonfiction, or they may be a creation of the author, called fiction. We'll talk more about these forms in Chapter 9. All narratives are plot-driven, including a sequence of events that create tensions and push the story along.

Types of Written Narrative

Most written narratives follow one of two patterns: either the classic narrative arc, or the "slice of life" piece.

Model 1: The Narrative Arc

In the classic narrative structure, the narrative begins slowly, picks up speed, builds to an arching climax, and then resolves. Let's look at each of these components in detail.

In the Beginning: Many stories begin *in medias res*, Latin for "in the middle of things." Because of this abrupt beginning, an important task in writing narrative is the creation of "backstory." Through backstory, the writer explains what happened before the story started. Think of this as the "once upon a time" phase.

Foreshadowing: Foreshadowing occurs when the writer provides a warning or hint of something that will happen later in the narrative. To be most effective, the foreshadowing must be subtle enough to not be obvious, yet visible enough to be picked up by the reader. Foreshadowing is a common technique in fiction and narrative nonfiction.

Conflict and the Rising Action: From its beginning, the story moves along and picks up momentum. Elements, characters, settings, and props may change or the writer may introduce new components or problems as a means of creating tension and conflict: a personal struggle or battle between opposing forces, or against some sort of obstacle. Conflict drives the narrative via an upward building of suspense known as the rising action.

Crisis: The story reaches a peak of action—a moment of maximum tension referred to as the story's crisis or climax. The crisis point may include surprises—as in the infamous plot twist—or may bring together existing characters and plot points to create some sort of change, or the "aha moment."

Resolution: Once the crisis point is past, tension resolves and the narrative arc tips downward in a phase known as resolution or denouement. Life within the story returns to a baseline state.

The Heroic Quest. The heroic quest or heroic journey is a special kind of narrative that threads through world literature, from ancient mythology to modern fantasy. The scholar and writer Joseph Campbell is known for the work he did on unifying the worldwide mythological description of the heroic quest and for identifying its wide occurrence throughout civilization. Here's the traditional quest model:

The hero (usually an adolescent male on the cusp of sexual maturity) . . .
  Rises to a heroic challenge that . . .
    Requires him to leave home in order to . . .
      Descend into a metaphoric underworld, a dark place of great danger, where . . .
        He does battle with some sort of monster (sometimes himself) . . .
          Which he usually wins . . .
            After which he leaves the darkness behind and . . .
              Returns to his people as . . .
                A wiser, mature version of his former self, who is . . .
                  Treated in kingly fashion as a wise elder and . . .
                  Placed in a leadership position and . . .
                    Showered with wealth and good fortune and he. . .
                      Lives happily ever after and . . .
                      Gets the girl.

*W*RITER'S
GRIMOIRE
In a novel or book-length memoir, each chapter has its own smaller version of the narrative arc, complete with the usual components.

Many works of magickal fiction correspond with the quest model: for example, the lead characters in the Harry Potter, Wizard of Earthsea, and Lord of the Rings series are all questing heroes.

Model 2: The Slice of Life

The slice-of-life piece looks like a chain, with scenes, recollections, or other anecdotes—short, amusing, or interesting stories—linked together in order to reach a point-of-end meaning. The anecdote-based piece often lacks a clear narrative arc but always includes an ultimate moment of realization (epiphany) for the central character(s).

PARTS OF THE STORY

Every story—spoken or written—includes theme, plot, characters, and setting. Together, these four structural elements provide a foundation for the narrative and bring it to life.

Theme

The theme of any story is its main idea. Theme may be stated outright, or it may be implied or hinted at by the characters, setting, and events in the story. A story's theme is its objective—it presents

*M*AGICKAL MENTION

Most ritual structure is like that of the traditional narrative arc. After a specific beginning or opening, magickal elements are introduced into the ritual, energy is created, and the intensity builds to a peak before resolving to a conclusion.

what readers would see as a universal or underlying truth, and it isn't designed to teach or moralize.

Plot

Plot is the way everything unfolds in a story—the way events and characters are revealed and the way in which they make things happen. Your story's plot may be linear, i.e., starting at one point in time and moving forward in time until a conclusion is reached. Or, it may move around in time via flashbacks, in which earlier or missing information is recalled, or via flash forwards, in which the writer may jump forward to explain or imagine an event that hasn't happened yet.

During the years I've studied writing, I've had several different teachers and mentors tell me that there are only two story plots: one, "a stranger comes to town," and two, "someone goes on a journey." This simple rule holds up well, although I find myself wanting to add a third possibility: "something unexpected (or magickal) happens."

Characters

Characters are the actors within your story—the ones who bring it to life. The process of characterization is the way a writer creates characters, introduces them, and puts them to work.

*M*AGICKAL
MENTION

Ritual also includes the same components as story. When planning a ritual, you create a theme for the event, determine the location, write or decide on the ritual's outline and content, and make lists of participants and materials needed.

Characterization may be **direct**—in which the writer tells the reader something specific about the character—or **indirect**, in which information about the character is revealed by the character herself or by other characters or events in the story. There are many ways to accomplish indirect characterization, including:

- dialogue

- description of the character's physical appearance, costume, etc.

- the character's activity and gestures

- the character's personality or quirks

- an understanding of the character's wishes and desires

- the ways the characters respond to each other

- the character's responses to situations and conflicts within the story

Character Structures

Within a story, the **protagonist** is the central character, the one who lives in the center of the story's conflict and drives the rising action. This is the character your readers will care about and follow through the story. In contrast, the **antagonist** is the person or force who opposes or works against the protagonist. The antagonist is sometimes a villain, but not always. In fact, the antagonist isn't always even human: it can also be a mythical monster, or a natural

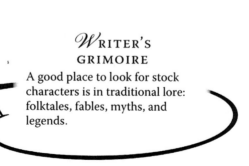

*W*RITER'S
GRIMOIRE
A good place to look for stock characters is in traditional lore: folktales, fables, myths, and legends.

force like a volcano. Some stories have more than one protagonist or antagonist. In the popular Lord of the Rings trilogy, Frodo and Sam are protagonists, Sauron and Mordor are antagonists, and Gollum manages to be both.

Dynamic characters change or are changed during the story, and they either cause or are involved with the story's rising action and climax. The more complex, ambivalent, or contradictory your characters, the greater their potential and the more interesting the story. **Static characters** stay the same throughout the story; nothing much happens to them and they don't advance the action—they're just sounding boards for the more active, dynamic characters. **Flat characters** exist to help support a scene or move the action along, but the reader knows and learns very little about them. **Round characters** are those that are essential to the story, and the reader knows and learns a great deal about them. Think of round characters as being, literally, three dimensional.

When creating characters and putting them to work, your minor characters must be written well enough to hold their own place and do whatever the story needs them to do without their elbowing their way in front of the focal players. Think of them as carrying around a torch to light the way for the leads. As for your major characters, most stories can't maintain more than a few of them at any one time. Imagine juggling: you can only keep so many chain saws in the air at once.

Whether your characters are fictional or real, you'll need to be familiar enough with them that you'll know how they would respond in any situation. Creating a character profile is one way to get to know them better:

Character's name:

Gender:

Age/birthday:

Physical size and appearance:

Ethnicity and background:

Character traits and personality:

Strengths and flaws:

Favorite foods and color:

Quirks and gestures:

Magickal practices and talents:

Pets and familiars:

Elemental association:

Favorite mode of transportation:

Typical attire:

One of the best moments in fiction writing is when a character says or does something that the writer neither planned nor expected. For a writer, this is pure gold, and the more complicated your characters are, the more likely it is to happen. Your knowledge of your story's players will help keep the writing complex and interesting, and it will also help you work against stereotypes. It's important that your characters aren't one-sided, for your reader won't believe in a character that is either too perfect or too evil. Your players must have their share of frailties, in terms of their physical or emotional natures. Also, while physical descriptions of characters are interesting, gestures are even better, and mannerisms and quirks are better yet. Ask yourself what the reader might *not* expect. Your protagonist might twist a magickal ring while thinking, might have a permanent tilt to their smile, a honking laugh, a fear of cheddar cheese, etc. Real people can be weird, so the weirder your characters are, the better.

Dialogue

Dialogue—the verbal interaction between or among characters—helps the reader understand the characters, the setting, and what's happening in the story. Good dialogue drives the plot and advances the action, and makes for a powerful reading experience as well. However, it's challenging to write good dialogue. In normal human conversation, our language is peppered with starts and stops, half-words, phrases, and shifts in meaning that may only make sense to the person speaking.

One of the best ways to learn dialogue is to spend time listening to the way real people speak. Settle yourself with pencil and paper in a place with lots of people—a coffee shop, city street, or local park—and wait to see and hear what happens around you. Listen to the people around you; capture bits of dialogue, write them down on paper, and later on study your notes, noticing patterns and examples that you can use for your characters' conversations. Read dialogue aloud to hear its sound and cadence. (An ethical note: If you find yourself inadvertently listening to something that becomes intensely personal, stop listening and turn your attention to a different conversation. Our goal in this exercise is to study the mechanics of dialogue—not eavesdrop.)

When writing dialogue:

1. Put quotation marks around each speaker's words. If the tag line comes before the quotation, put a comma after it, before the quotation marks.

    > The wizard <u>said</u>, "I didn't hear the doorbell. I was taking a bath."

2. If the tag line comes after the quotation, put a comma inside the final quotation mark if the quotation ends with a period. If the quotation ends with a question mark or exclamation mark, skip the comma.

    > "I didn't hear the doorbell. I was taking a bath," the wizard <u>said</u>.

3. If the tag line falls in the middle of the quotation, place a comma before it inside the quotation marks and after it, before the quotation marks.

    > "I didn't hear the doorbell," the wizard <u>said</u>, "because I was taking a bath."

4. Start a new paragraph whenever someone new starts talking, or if a speaker is still talking but switches topics.

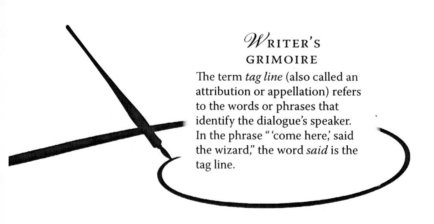

*W*RITER'S GRIMOIRE

The term *tag line* (also called an attribution or appellation) refers to the words or phrases that identify the dialogue's speaker. In the phrase " 'come here,' said the wizard," the word *said* is the tag line.

(In that case, omit the closing quotation mark on the first paragraph, but begin the new paragraph with an opening quotation mark.) Indent the start of each new paragraph.

5. The word *said* is always the best tag line, since readers are trained early on to simply read over the word, catching its meaning without breaking the flow of dialogue. If using other tags—"he exclaimed," "she explained"—keep them to a minimum, especially within adjacent lines.
    Not so good:

    > "What do you think we should do?" <u>posed</u> Jim, questioningly.
    > "I have no idea," <u>retorted</u> Mark, worriedly.

    Better:

    > "What do you think we should do?" <u>asked</u> Jim.
    > "I have no idea," <u>said</u> Mark.

In the second example, we also dumped the adverbs. Leave most adverbs out of dialogue! Adverbs are words that modify verbs, explaining where, when, or how an action is taking place. Most adverbs are easily spotted, as they end in -ly. Many writers sprinkle their prose with adverbs. The problem is that adverbs often weaken a sentence rather than strengthening it. How? First, adverbs tend to coerce the reader into taking a specific view or feeling a certain emotion.

Weak:

> "Where are we?" asked Jim, rubbing his head fearfully.

Stronger:

> "Where are we?" asked Jim, rubbing his head.

By using *fearfully*, the writer tries to strong-arm us into deciding Jim is afraid. We'll engage better with the story if we're allowed to understand the fear by reading into the scene and figuring out that Jim's in danger.

Second, adverbs are often redundant, repeating connotations or meanings we can infer from other words or phrases.

Weak:

"Ouch!" Mark yelped, jerking his hand back quickly.

Stronger:

"Ouch!" Mark yelped, jerking his hand back.

Quickly is unnecessary; Mark jerked his hand back, and we already know that a jerking movement is quick.

Not all adverbs are evil:

Mark put one hand up to the void and pushed it through tentatively. His hand disappeared into nothing.

In the above sample, it would be difficult to replace the adverb *tentatively* without adding several words and losing the impact of the short, crisp sentence. *Suddenly* is another adverb that does a lot of work in a sentence and is often worth keeping. To decide if an adverb is helping or hindering, read the sentence aloud, with and without the adverb. If you aren't 100 percent convinced that it should remain, get rid of it or replace it with a stronger image.

Special Techniques with Dialogue

To reveal more about your characters, try some of these special effects. Many of these pop up often in magickal and fantasy writing, where they lend flavor to the words. They're also useful in spells and ritual, when clever vocal techniques bring the magick to life.

- *Diction*: the way character chooses and uses her words. For example, an educated character—such as an elder wizard, or a key player in an important ritual—might speak with exaggerated, complex diction:

"I prefer to use a magickal wand with the utmost respect that it is due, given its lofty status as an instrument of personal power and absolute precision."

On the other hand, a child character might speak with short sentences, and simple diction:

"I wish I had a magick wand. I would use it to work spells. I would change my brother into a toad."

- *Jargon*: a special vocabulary used by a particular group. Jargon is interesting, but using it without explanation creates a frustrated, confused reader. If using jargon, be sure to embed the meaning in your writing so the reader can follow along.

The coven gathered in a circle, hands clasped.
"Since we're banishing, we'll do the spiral dance widdershins," explained the Priestess, pulling the line of people into a slow walk behind her.

*M*AGICKAL MENTION

- A besom is a magickal broom.

- Widdershins refers to a circle being cast or followed to the left, or counterclockwise (also called sun-wise); deosil refers to casting or following to the right, or clockwise.

- Warding is a kind of defensive magick that deflects danger, while banishing removes negative energy.

- A spiral dance is a ritual group activity in which celebrants dance in a spiraling line.

Banishing? Spiral dance? thought Spudfern, who had no idea what the words meant. *I thought we were doing a ritual to dissolve a hex? And why are we walking counter-clockwise?*

- *Euphemism*: a mild or indirect expression that replaces a harsh, blunt, or embarrassing word; also used to bestow a fond nickname.

  Nonmagickal folk may be referred to as "muggles" or "mundies." Faeries, brownies, and their kin may be called "the wee folk."

- *Slang*: words and phrases that are regarded as rough or informal and used within a specific group of people. A good example in the magickal and electronic worlds is the use of "newbie" to describe someone who is new to a place or set of practices.

Setting

The story's setting is the backdrop for its characters, the place in which the events take place. Setting may be created in two ways:

- By giving the reader a direct description of the surroundings:

  It was a dark and stormy night.

  (By the way—although attributed to the famous canine novelist known as Snoopy, this line was penned circa 1830 by the English novelist Edward Bulwer-Lytton.)

- By having the reader observe an interaction between character and setting. This could include dialogue or thoughts:

  He heard the sound of the great forest, the wind whistling through the ancient firs, adding to the already foreboding aspect. The dark forest was safer than the main road, but tales of werewolves and other less human creatures stirred the hairs on his neck.

Setting may include some or all of these elements: descriptions of place, date, season, weather, scenic elements, or people who are present; allusions to the passing of time; and symbolic elements. It may accomplish some or all of the following:

- setting the scene, i.e., introducing the story's location or starting point

- setting tone, mood, and atmosphere

- affecting the story's level of realism, either making it more or less realistic

- creating a natural force that opposes the protagonist

- reinforcing behavior of the characters

- reinforcing other story elements

In some stories, setting is simply a backdrop. In others, it becomes important to the story itself or plays an active role in the story. Remember the apple trees in *Wizard of Oz*—the ones that come to life and start pelting Dorothy with fruit, adding to the sense of violence and foreboding?

In general, the more sensory detail given about a setting, the more intimate it feels. Word choice becomes important: using a lot of words with specific emotional connotations (positive, negative, light-hearted, frightening, etc.) creates specific kinds of tone and mood within the implied location.

The above discussion of setting is described in terms of crafting a story or piece of narrative. Setting plays a similar role in your magickal workings and ritual, and has many of the same functions. Think about how some rituals may be suited to sunny outdoor settings, while others flow better in a dark, enclosed space.

OTHER STORY ELEMENTS

The Power of the First Line

As a story's writer, you have a powerful opportunity to draw in your reader and make him take what writers refer to as "the hook." This grand opportunity happens in the story's first line, where your carefully chosen words can make or break a reader's decision to keep reading or move on to other texts. Here are a few first lines from well-known magickal stories:

> "When Mr. Bilbo Baggins of Bag End announced that he would shortly be celebrating his eleventy-first birthday with a party of special magnificence, there was much talk and excitement in Hobbiton."
>
> —*Lord of the Rings: The Fellowship of the Ring*, J. R. R. Tolkein

> "The Island of Gont, a single mountain that lifts its peak a mile above the storm-wracked Northeast Sea, is a land famous for wizards."
>
> —*A Wizard of Earthsea*, Ursula K. Le Guin

> "Wind howled through the night, carrying a scent that would change the world."
>
> —*Eragon*, Christopher Paolini

> "The storm had broken."
>
> —*Magician: Apprentice*, Raymond E. Feist

A good first line should be fun to read and engaging, making the reader interested and curious and leading her to want more. Make your first lines count.

Symbolism

A symbol is a person, place, thing, or idea that suggests something beyond its literal meaning. Magick folks are used to symbols and use them every day: consider, for example, runic symbols, tarot cards, or an inscribed pentagram.

A symbol may contain multiple meanings—either by resemblance, by pattern of appearance, or through longstanding relationships to mythology, archetypes, etc.—and those meanings may be literal or metaphorical. In writing, symbols support the plot and may give the characters something to do; even more, the use of symbols becomes a set of clues that weaves the theme throughout the story.

Some symbols are so entrenched in modern literature that they come with ready-made meanings:

- When a **ship** appears, a character is about to take a journey.

- If a character comes to a **crossroad**, **veil**, or **threshold**, they're standing on the brink of a decision or movement into an unknown place.

- When the **moon** comes out, especially the full moon, a sense of mystery is afoot.

- If a character is **immersed in water** and emerges, suspect baptism, rebirth, or transformation until proven otherwise.

- The **seasons** almost always have specific meanings: spring is a time of rebirth, new beginnings, and initiation; summer is all about fecundity and life at its fullest expression; autumn reflects a time of harvest, fading, or winding down; winter invokes death, solitude, and waiting.

Other symbols are even less obvious, often alluding to mythological, cultural, or religious topics. These are wonderful additions to your magickal practices. For example, a Wiccan storyteller who uses Salem as a setting is alluding to "the burning times." The recurrence of the mythological phoenix in the Harry Potter books echoes a theme of resurrection and rebirth that wends its way through the seven volumes.

Magick is also full of symbolism. For example, we use chalice and blade in ritual to symbolize the Great Rite of sexual communion between the archetypal male and female. We use the pentagram symbol to show the four cardinal elements and the fifth element, spirit.

Parable and Allegory

Parable and allegory often pop up in heroic quests, fables, mythology, and written narratives, as well as in magickal ritual, song, and storytelling.

A **parable** is a simple story used to illustrate an explicit (obvious) moral or spiritual lesson. In the myth of Icarus, his wax and feather wings melt when his vanity pushes him to fly too close to the sun; as a result, his bigger mission fails, his father perishes, and Icarus himself falls to Earth and dies. The lesson? Something along the lines of pride going before a really big fall.

An **allegory** is a piece of writing that can be interpreted to reveal an implicit hidden meaning, most often a moral or political message. Many scholars believe that J. R. R. Tolkien's Lord of the Rings trilogy was written as an allegory of the tragedy and needless suffering endured during World War I.

The Writer's Eye

One of my teachers once told me that writers can see things that other people can't, and they can write about those things in a way that helps the other people see them. As a writer, work to develop your writer's eye. Prowl for stories. Look for the startling, the unusual, the absurd, the gorgeous, the unspoken. The world is full of complexities and contradictions: look at a piano teacher, a hiker, and a librarian, but *see* the piano teacher who flies on the back of a dragon by night, the hiker who stumbles upon a spring that confers immortality hidden within deep woods, the librarian who is part of a millennia old sisterhood, guarding the Book of Thoth in the Everytown Municipal Library. Paint rich characters with odd gestures, unexpected hobbies, raspy voices, and hungry pets with long, sharp teeth.

 _____

1. Create a one-paragraph setting of your choice. Load it with descriptive words and phrases that convey darkness, danger, gloom, fear, etc. Reread your work: were you successful in setting the tone of the paragraph? Repeat the exercise, using words that signify light, safety, optimism, and hope.

2. Here's a fun way to come up with creative character descriptions. Start with a blank piece of paper. On one side, create a long list of magickal persons, animals, creatures, etc. On the other side, create a list of random, mundane actions. Mix and match items from each list and see what kinds of characters emerge. Example:

Bard	lit sparklers
Bat	scattered daisies
Bookworm	made fudge
Dragon	mowed the lawn
Druid	knit socks
Herbalist	walked a tightrope
Witch	swam a moat
Wizard	ordered Chinese food

Imagine the magickal little character you could create around a dragon who mows his lawn!

eight

THE WRITER'S VOICE

So what is a writer's "voice"? Voice is the writer's shade, a spirit-presence that echoes through one's work, a simmering brew of the narrator's persona and the craft elements used to create the work. Voice is what engages a reader and carries them through a piece. It's voice that sets the mood and makes a story thrilling, causing a reader to either race through it because it is so compelling they can't bear to set it down, or to limit themselves to reading only a few pages a day, so the story—and the voice—don't come to an end one moment sooner than they must.

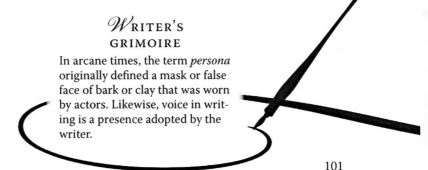

Writer's GRIMOIRE

In arcane times, the term *persona* originally defined a mask or false face of bark or clay that was worn by actors. Likewise, voice in writing is a presence adopted by the writer.

Voice is arguably *the* most important aspect of writing—and yet it's one of the hardest concepts to nail down. Ask a host of writers to define voice and you'll receive an equal number of varied answers, none right or wrong, but all a little different. To complicate things further, voice is often described in the same breath as style, tone, and point of view, yet without specifying how the different terms are related, or even *if* they're related.

My favorite definition of voice is the one offered by writer Tim Schell in his text, *Mooring Against the Tide*. Schell suggests that the terms *style*, *tone*, and *voice* are too often used interchangeably by writers and readers. He describes the following relationship between the terms:

Style + Tone = Voice

This equation holds true where . . .

- *Style* is the way a writer uses language: the way she chooses words, varies sentence length, uses imagery, chooses a point of view, selects punctuation, etc. Style also includes the way a writer matches her work to her audience.

- *Tone* is the way that the writer uses techniques like irony, understatement, sarcasm, and hyperbole to create a mood. When we read a piece of writing and feel a strong sensation or feeling in response to it, we've fallen subject to the piece's tone, or mood.

Why do I like Schell's definition? It's concrete, reasonable, and offers a formula to help any writer—especially a "young" writer—think about the components of style, tone, and voice, and how they work together. Schell's definition may not be perfect, but it's a great place to begin. At the very least, it will help you think about what creates voice and how you might experiment with the process.

Writers hone their voice over time through experience and practice, each finding their own unique ways of being present in the work. An aficionado of J. R. R. Tolkien, Ray Bradbury, or Edgar Allan Poe would be able to pick up one of that author's stories and know within a few lines who had written it, based on voice alone. For beginning writers, a good starting rule is this: your writing should "sound" reasonably like your normal speech, or close to it. For example, if you'd normally voice a thought like this—"I'm going to spend some time working with crystals"—you wouldn't write the same thought as, "I have decided to engage in an in-depth, substantive examination of homogeneous solid substances with natural geometrically regular forms and symmetrically arranged plane faces." It just wouldn't sound like your voice.

Magickal Rhetoric

Rhetoric is the art of persuasion, either spoken or written, and a rhetorical strategy is the way a writer crafts her work to make it connect with a specific audience. This isn't as highfalutin as it sounds—we use rhetoric every day. If you received a speeding ticket and wrote a letter to the judge asking for lenience, you'd be polite, respectful, and chagrined, with apologetic language and a formally structured, typed letter. If, on the other hand, you were writing your favorite aunt to ask if she'd help you sew a new set of ritual robes, you'd likely handwrite a newsy letter with a warm familiar tone, and you might slip in a photograph or two. In each letter, you'd have different goals and you'd use different rhetorical strategies to achieve them.

Consider the following examples of how we use rhetoric in our magickal practices:

- Most guided meditations are reflective, conversational, and free flowing. They're usually written in an intimate, soothing voice that sets a comfortable tone and encourages participation.

- Highly ritualized or important spellwork tends to use formal language and either spoken dialogue, chant, or ritual poetry.

The formality becomes an important aspect of the magick and creates a mood reflecting the serious intent.

- A ritual designed for a specific purpose—warding, banishing, protection, etc.—often includes stylized elements and a precise vocabulary. If you're invoking Brigid, you use her name; you wouldn't call upon "that Celtic goddess who hangs around the fireplace."

- A joyous Mabon feast might be spontaneous and unrehearsed; a ritual feast could be carefully choreographed; and a dumb supper at Samhain might have no spoken words at all, and yet use a written, detailed outline.

In each example, the choice of structural and stylistic elements and the creation of a specific tone yields a unique voice that matches and supports the magickal intention.

Point of View

Every piece of writing has a speaker—the narrator—and that speaker's voice creates the story's point of view (POV). Writers choose a specific point of view to contain their work and determine how it is conveyed to the audience. There are three main points of view:

*M*AGICKAL
MENTION

- Mabon is one of the names for celebration and rituals associated with the autumnal equinox.

- The dumb supper is a silent meal held to honor the dead and departed.

- First person: *"I waved the wand."* This is the most intimate view, as we're in the narrator's head and know what she's saying. When we call the quarters in ritual, we typically speak in first person:

  > "I call upon you, guardians of the north, keepers of stone and story, of Earth's permanence, home of winter's sleep. I invite you to be here, now!"

- Second person: *"You waved the wand."* The person leading a guided meditation often uses second person to symbolically direct the action:

  > "You are walking through a forest. Light streams through openings in the canopy above. The air is cool and sweet. You can hear rushing water some distance away. You breathe deeply. A sense of peace flows through you."

- Third person: *"He waved the wand."* The perspective isn't very intimate, but it gives a wide-angle view and lots of information about what's happening. When writing a report—for example, for a course of "year and a day" studies—one's words are usually in an objective third person:

  > "Like the candle, the volcano displays all four elements at once: earth in the rock that comprises and is formed by the volcanic action; air in the gasses that vent from the crater, and the way that rock and lava are ejected into the air; fire in the molten rock that moves beneath Earth's surface; and water in the steam plumes that issue from the volcano."

Stream of Consciousness

Stream of consciousness is a special narrative technique in which thoughts and sensory impressions are presented as if they're coming directly from the narrator's or a character's mind. The ideas flow as normal thoughts flow; in other words, they don't necessarily come in linear fashion, they feel jumpy and fragmented, and they don't follow a logical pattern. Stream of consciousness narrative is a powerful way to reveal a character's inner thoughts, personality, and emotional status. In magickal writing, stream of consciousness works well when the writer wishes to convey meditation, trance, astral travel, magickal control, or entrance into magickal realms.

Word Choice

As a writer, you only have a few physical tools at your disposal; pen, paper (or laptop), and words are the most important. Good word choice is an important aspect of your writing, and you'll want to make sure that every word on the page does as much work as it can. Aim for vivid, exciting language. For instance, why run if you can sprint or dash? Why eat if you can devour or consume? Why recite if you can incant? Use your thesaurus to search for uncommon, dynamic words to spice up your writing. This is especially important in spellwork, where finding the *perfect* word can be a marvelous addition to the spell or charm and can even make your magick all the more powerful.

 *Scribbulus* _____

1. What does the idea of voice mean to you, right now? Free-write or create an entry in your writing journal. Sign and date it. Come back to the entry in two or three months, read it, and add fresh thoughts and comments. Watch this idea as it evolves over time.

2. Write a short scene or anecdote using a first person point of view. Then, rewrite it in third person. Consider the differences between the two. Which one sounds better to your ear? Which do you like better? Which works best for the piece of writing?

3. See how many synonyms you can find for the following words:

charm	study
essay	tone
journal	voice
magick	Witch
story	

nine

A Grimoire of Traditional Writing

Have you ever yearned to write a fantasy novel, submit an essay to a Pagan publication, or even set down your own life story as Witch or wizard? While we don't have the time or space in this book for a complete magickal writing course, I'd like to give you an overview of the more common traditional writing forms. If you don't feel the need to learn more about these now, skip ahead to Chapter 10. Otherwise, join me for a quick look at the spectrum of fiction and nonfiction writing.

FICTION

Fiction is creative writing based on "made-up" or historical characters, places, and events. Fictional writing comes in a wide range of genres (science fiction, mystery, fantasy, etc.) and in all shapes and sizes. The novel is a book-length work of fiction, usually upwards of 40,000 words. The novella (or novelette) is shorter than a novel and longer than a short story. A short story usually runs 8,000 words or fewer, while a short-short, ultrashort, or flash story—a *very* brief work of fiction—typically has fewer than 500 words.

If you're interested in writing fiction, these ideas will help you begin:

- Who is your audience?

- What will your story be about? What is its central theme or idea? What point are you trying to make with the story?

- Who is the story's narrator?

- Does your tale have a clear beginning, middle, and end?

- How long will your piece be? A short story? A novel?

- You'll need a protagonist and antagonist. And what about other main characters? Minor characters?

- Will you use symbolism?

- What is the story's central conflict? How will it be resolved?

- Where does the story take place? What is the setting?

- Which point of view will you use to tell the story?

- How will you add magick to the piece?

*W*RITER'S
GRIMOIRE
The graphic novel is one whose story is conveyed primarily through illustrations.

NONFICTION

Nonfiction encompasses a broad range of writing, from personal narrative to academic writing to journalism to folkloric legend.

Personal Narrative

Personal narrative writing explores human relationships and finds common patterns and magickal threads hidden among them. Personal narratives always have two layers: a surface (obvious) meaning, and a deeper (undiscovered) meaning. In the process of discovering the deeper meaning, a change in understanding—a kind of magickal transformation—occurs between writer and reader.

There are three main types of personal narrative: memoir, personal essay, and the previously discussed *sub rosa* work (see Chapter 1).

The Memoir

The word *memoir* is from the French *mémoire*, literally, "memory." A memoir is a nonfiction work based on a memory—a recalled segment of a person's life—as written by that person. Through excavation of

*W*RITER'S
GRIMOIRE

The word *author*—one who writes or creates a work of prose—comes from the Old French *autorite*, from Latin *auctoritas*, meaning "originator" or "promoter." To have authority is to speak with the strength of creation, and that which is authentic is considered genuine, i.e., authoritative—from the mouth (or pen) of the author.

and reflection on the memory, the writer discovers hidden meanings and comes to a point of greater self-understanding. Memoir pieces may vary in length from short pieces to book-length works. A well-known magickal memoir is Phyllis Curott's *Witch Crafting*.

The Personal Essay

The personal essay is a true, essay-length work in which the writer uses her personal experiences to explore a larger idea, question, or problem. During this process, the writer's insights are revealed and her opinions and emotions come together to shape a new, deeper understanding. Many of the essays that we read in Pagan publications, or on message sites such as *Witchvox*, are personal essays.

Time-Driven Narrative

The time-driven work is organized chronologically and encompasses two main types: biography and autobiography. The biography is a time-driven story of a person's entire life, written by someone else via a third person point of view. The autobiography is a time-driven story of a person's entire life, written by that person via a first per-

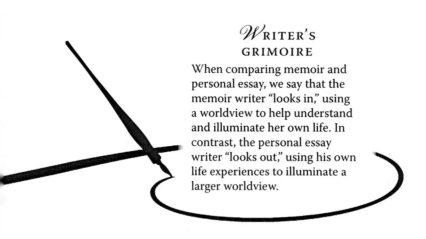

*W*RITER'S GRIMOIRE

When comparing memoir and personal essay, we say that the memoir writer "looks in," using a worldview to help understand and illuminate her own life. In contrast, the personal essay writer "looks out," using his own life experiences to illuminate a larger worldview.

son point of view. The goal is the arranging of a life on paper, and a linear mapping of the central character's movement through that life from beginning to end. In contrast, memoir is a memory-driven story of a specific episode or time from a person's life, as written by that person, usually in a first person point of view.

Academic Narrative

When you think of academic writing, think of school. This is the kind of objective prose that help us write essays, research papers, reports, etc. If you're an initiate or apprentice in a magickal tradition, you may be asked to prepare written summaries or reports of your work. Or, you might be interested in crafting essays to turn into journalistic pieces for submission to a magickal media market.

The Essay

An essay is a story-length piece of writing on a particular subject. The word comes from the Old French *essai,* "trial," and essays try to teach, tell, or persuade; some do a combination of all three. As

*W*RITER'S GRIMOIRE

Don't confuse "writing a memoir" with the idea of "writing one's memoirs." Certain people—business magnates, political figures, royalty, etc.—often settle down in their retirement years to "write their memoirs." What they're actually crafting is more akin to a linear autobiography than true memoir.

a form of prose, the essay is credited to Michel de Montaigne, a French renaissance scholar who merged scholarly writing with personal anecdote and opinion and came up with something entirely new, laying the groundwork for the future of nonfiction writing.

A traditional essay has three parts:

- the introduction, with the central idea (thesis) that drives the piece

- the body, with two or more paragraphs used to discuss the essay's content

- the conclusion, in which the work is summarized and brought to a thoughtful close

Argumentative essays—those that seek to establish or prove a position—also use a central claim and support that claim with evidence.

The Research Paper

The research paper is an in-depth exploration of a research question or topic. By researching the material, critiquing available scholarship, and synthesizing one's own position, the writer enters into a wide academic discussion about the topic.

The research paper usually contains these structural components:

- an introduction, including the central research question or hypothesis driving the piece (often called a thesis statement)

- a section for review or backstory, in which the writer summarizes current knowledge and work on the subject

- an introduction of findings, questions, or insights

- a discussion and synthesis of the above

- a conclusion

- a bibliography of sources and materials used in the paper

Journalism

Traditional journalism—what we read in newspapers and maga-zines—is a structured form that involves in-depth research, report-ing, and intentional objectivity: "just the facts, ma'am." Photojour-nalism uses photographs or images to tell some or all of the story.

Literary journalism is a kind of creative nonfiction that springs from traditional journalism. Sometimes called "immersion journal-ism" or "new journalism," literary journalism is an essay- or book-length work of nonfiction in which a narrator takes a close, detailed look at a person, place, event, or idea. Like traditional journalism, the work involves research and journalistic reporting. But in lit-erary journalism, the perspective is via the narrator's eye, and the narrator bundles the information into a fascinating story. One of the magickal community's best-known pieces of literary journalism is Margot Adler's seminal *Drawing Down the Moon.*

*M*AGICKAL
MENTION

The hypothesis, which literally means "under the foundation," is a proposed explanation used as a starting point for investiga-tion. Magick is also all about hypothesis. When you work with a new spell or ritual, tweak the components of a potion, etc., you're creating a fresh hypothesis and conducting your own mini research project.

OTHER KINDS OF PROSE:
POETRY, POETIC NARRATIVE, AND DRAMATIC NARRATIVE

A poem is a literary work in which special effort is given to the expression of feelings and ideas through the use of distinctive style, rhythm, structure, and figurative language. Some longer poems tell a story and are thus narratives; a good example is the epic poem, e.g., *Dante's Inferno*. Other poems simply capture an emotion or a moment in time.

Drama (dramatic narrative) refers to a play written for radio, television, film, or theater. Conducted mainly through staging and dialogue, dramatic narrative may be live—as in live stage performances—or recorded and time-delayed.

We'll touch on poetry writing in Chapter 15. If you're interested in deeper exploration of these forms, check the Resources section for materials.

*Scribbulus*

1. Dedicate a writing journal page to your favorite short stories. Note the name of each story, its writer, and a brief synopsis. Think about why each story appeals to you. How does each writer use his or her special vision to show you something you didn't see on your own?

2. Use your writing journal to start a list of possible essay topics. As time allows, use invention methods to explore one or more topics.

3. As noted above, the memoir is written about a recalled segment from one's life. If you were going to craft a memoir piece about your life, what portion or segment would you choose? Freewrite on this idea, and see what surfaces.

ten

A Grimoire of Magickal Writing

In this chapter, we'll look at magickal documents from antiquity to modern times. While some of these haven't been seen for centuries, each is full of possibilities. A few of these forms aren't inherently magickal but can work especially well for magickal purposes. Fasten your pointy hat and get ready to explore!

Almanac

An annual calendar containing important dates and statistical information, such as astronomical data and tide tables. Many magickal and mundane versions are available today.

Bestiary

Bestiaries were medieval books of animal lore. Heavily illustrated, a bestiary described the nature and habits of animals both real and fabled, and attached symbolic moral and religious meanings to each animal. Most bestiaries were based on the fourth-century Greek

Physiologus, a natural history text believed to have been compiled at Alexandria around the second century CE. The animal symbolism within bestiaries was used to create the fables, parables, and allegories that influenced medieval intellectual life.

Book of Changes

The Chinese Book of Changes, or *I Ching*, is actually one of a set of five sacred books constructed of sixty-four related hexagrams, along with commentaries attributed to Confucius. The Book of Changes creates divination readings via a system of symbols, poems, and related commentary, and describes all human interactions in terms of the interaction of yin and yang.

Book of the Dead

The Book of the Dead is a funerary text from ancient Egypt. While not believed to be a religious text, the book explains and gives detailed instructions about the mystical nature of the afterlife, including charms and spells to help the soul find its way to the underworld. For the Tibetan Book of the Dead, see page 127.

Book of Hours

A traditional Book of Hours was an ornate, illuminated medieval text containing the prayers or offices to be recited at the day's canonical hours. Books of Hours mostly belonged to the wealthy.

Book of Lights

Some practitioners feel that "Book of Shadows" is a dark, somewhat forbidding term. Wanting to distinguish their own practices as being full of light and beneficent magick, they have coined the term "Book of Lights" as an alternative.

Book of Raziel

The Book of Raziel is a spell book, supposedly written by an angel and given to the biblical Adam after his eviction from Eden.

Book of Shadows

A Book of Shadows (BOS) is a sacred book of ritual, magickal lore, spells, chants, divination, and other arcane practices. Historically, covens kept their own Book of Shadows to record their secret rites and teachings; these were kept safe by a designated high priest or priestess, and passed down for decades or even centuries. Today, many individual magickal practitioners keep their own personal Book of Shadows—most are still handwritten, but many are now kept on laptops and CDs as well. The keeping of the Book of Shadows has, in itself, become a kind of tradition that connects modern magickal practitioners with their medieval brethren. Many of these books today are works of art.

Book of Signs

This book was given to the Etruscans (the people of ancient, pre-Roman Italy and Corsica) by a mysterious being called Tages; the book would form the basis of the Etruscans' spiritual traditions, which focused in immanent polytheism and the idea that all visible or perceptive phenomena were expressions of divine power.

Book of Simples

A Book of Simples is a personal collection of herbal recipes and combinations. In herbal terms, a "simple" is a brew or infusion that uses a single herbal ingredient (e.g., simple syrup of sugar and water used in beverage making). The Book of Simples name is an affectionate reference to an herbalist's own cookbook.

Book of Thoth

This famous ancient Egyptian tome is said to be a complete revelation of the world's most sacred spells—those that could freeze the Sun in the sky, or keep the Earth from turning. No one knows what became of the Book of Thoth itself. Some legends suggest it was intentionally destroyed; others say that it is hidden in Egypt, awaiting discovery. "Thoth" may be pronounce like "tote" (rhymes with boat) or "thoath" (rhymes with oath) (*American Heritage Dictionary*).

Chapbook

A chapbook is an informal "collection" of writing, usually made by folding standard sheets of paper in half and stapling the sheets at the center to form a simple "book" of blank pages. Chapbooks are usually thematic, often focusing on poetry collections. Many writers and poets share their work through chapbooks, which are easy and inexpensive to make. For this reason, they're also a favorite quick publication form for magickal writers.

Codex

A codex is a handwritten book dating from late antiquity or the early Middle Ages. Codexes were formed with a group of pages bound between wooden (and later, stiff vellum or parchment) covers; these books represented a significant improvement over scrolls, for codexes could be opened flat, allowing one to write on both sides of the page. Many magickal practitioners today craft their own codex books, large or small, feeling that this adds greatly to their magickal practices (see Chapter 17).

Corpus Hermeticum

Composed of fifteen to eighteen tractates (different sources group the texts in different ways), the *Corpus*—literally "body"—comprises core documents of the Hermetic tradition. The Hermetica is a mystery tradition usually attributed to Hermes Trismegistus, a merging of the Greek Hermes (associated with commerce, invention, and cunning; also known as the messenger of the gods) and the Egyptian Thoth (legendary author of books on magick, alchemy, and astrology). Hermetic beliefs encompass religion, philosophy, and occult magick, and included early expressions of the four elements, theurgy, and the relationship of energy to magick.

E-Book

The e-book is an electronic version of a printed book that can be read on a personal computer or hand-held device designed specifically for this purpose. Many magickal books—fiction and nonfiction—are available as e-books.

Emerald Tablet

The Emerald Tablet is an ancient text said to hold the secrets of the primordial substance, the secrets of immortality, and the acts of transmutation (both of solid metals and of the human soul). It is said to be the work of Hermes Trismegistus, an Egyptian sage supposedly inspired by the Egyptian god Thoth, the Greek god Hermes, or perhaps both. The Emerald Tablet is considered to be a foundational text of traditional alchemy and ceremonial magick.

Ephemeris

The ephemeris is a table or data set giving the calculated positions of celestial objects; also used to describe nature-based or taxonomic information. Ephemera today are found in magickal and mundane almanacs.

Formulary

A formulary is a collection of formulas or set ritual forms for use in religious ceremonies. This sort of formulary is often included in a Book of Shadows. The word can also refer to a written collection describing the actions and details of medicines. Many herbologists and magickal healers develop and keep their own formularies.

Grimoire

A grimoire is a grammar of magickal spells, traditions, and inspirations. The typical grimoire is a "how to" book of techniques and processes, rather than a repository of specific lore and secrets.

Herbarium

An herbarium is a book-mounted collection of actual dried herbs and plants, along with textual information about their uses in healing. The specimens may be whole plants or plant parts. In medieval times, herbaria were invaluable in the study and identification of plants and the training of health care providers.

Historia

A historia is a time-based treatise of human history or natural history. The earliest historias would eventually become the modern history books. Today, magicians who study lore and mythology may create historias that resemble those of olden times.

Leechbook

A leechbook is an herbarium that also includes the superstitious, magickal, and/or healing uses of herbs and plants. Find a leechbook and a wise herbalist won't be far behind.

Materia

A materia is an encyclopedic collection of information on a general subject. For example, *De Materia Medica,* compiled by the Greek physician Pedanius Dioscorides, featured information on medicinal plants.

Mutus Liber

The *Mutus Liber,* the "mute book" or "silent book" of alchemy, is a wordless book containing fifteen illustration-plates of alchemical processes. Said to have been created in 1677 by author Jacob Sulat, the images supposedly capture the steps involved in creating the Philosopher's Stone.

On-Demand Publishing

On-demand publishing, an offshoot of the electronic publishing industry, is the process by which a manuscript is uploaded to an Internet host and then may be printed when purchased or ordered by a customer. This differs from traditional publishing, in which a set number of books—usually at least several hundred—are printed all at one time and then marketed to customers. On-demand publishing has made it possible for many magick writers to publish works that would ordinarily be declined by mainstream publishers.

Online (Electronic) Publications

An online publication is any written work that is published exclusively electronically, usually on the Internet.

Periodicals

A periodical is a magazine, newspaper, newsletter, or gazette that includes topical content and is published at regular intervals. Today's magickal community is lucky to have available a wide variety of these traditional publications, running the gamut from local newspapers and newsletters to nationally published magazines.

Pharmacopeia

A pharmacopeia lists medicines and herbs with their effects and directions for use. The term may also reference a stock of medicinal drugs. Both of these usages go back to medieval times, where monks sequestered themselves within cloistered communities and maintained age-old herbal traditions. Magickal and herbal healers still use pharmacopeias today, as do Western and Eastern pharmacies.

Prayer Book (Missal)

A prayer book is a text containing prayers, blessings, bestowals, music, and rituals used by individuals or as part of group religious practices. Many practicing Pagans and other magicians craft their own prayer books or place the contents as a section within their Book of Shadows.

Table of Houses

A Table of Houses is a set of tables giving signs and degrees for the house cusps as used to create and interpret horoscopes. The Table lists the zodiacal positions of the house cusps at different latitudes according to sidereal time. In Western astrology, the Table is expressed as a set of figures, arranged in columns to facilitate the

*M*AGICKAL
MENTION

Sidereal time is that which determines time with respect to the distant stars (i.e., the constellations or fixed stars) rather than to the sun or planets.

calculation of zodiacal degrees for the Ascendant, Midheaven, and the other houses' cusps. It is often packaged with other horoscopic ephemera, including the Table of Values, used for calculating planetary weighting or numerical value when assessing a horoscope.

Tibetan Book of the Dead

This text includes art and literature reflecting the prayer, ritual, and meditative death and afterlife traditions of Tibet, Nepal, and India. The correct name is *Bardo Thodol*, literally "liberation to liminality," reflecting the idea that death liberates the soul to a liminal space, where the soul awaits its next rebirth or reincarnation. A good general source for discussion of the Tibetan Book of the Dead can be found through the University of Virginia's library site: http://www2 .lib.virginia.edu/exhibits/dead/index2.html. An online translation of the text is available at: http://www.summum.us/mummification/ tbotd.

Zine

The zine (short for "magazine") is a kind of formal chapbook. Zines are soft-cover and usually produced with desktop publishing software. They model the format and structure of a magazine and may include artwork and advertisements. Many large bookstores keep a zine rack in their periodical section, and a number of writers have broken into the publishing industry by creating zines. The webzine or e-zine is an electronic version, published on the Internet. Because of its ease of use and "hominess," zines are a wonderful venue for magickal writers wanting to share their work.

Scribbulus

1. Does your magickal tradition work with a specific kind of text? See what you can find out about that text's history.

2. Review the list of texts above, and find one that intrigues you. Devote a page in your writing notebook to outlining how you might develop your own version of a historia, leechbook, or zine.

3. Imagine yourself finding an ancient text. You open the book . . . slowly. What do you find? Write an entry in your notebook about this imagined ancient text and what it means to you.

eleven

GOOD READING = GOOD WRITING

For writers, reading is both a form of enjoyment and one of study. When you read, you examine the craft of other writers. You study how they handle tricky characters, plot arcs, delicate endings, or moments of reflective insight. You experience different voices, styles, and techniques, and you'll find yourself inspired to try some of these out in your own writing. And here is an essential truth of becoming a good writer:

—To be a good writer, you must also be an active reader.—

WHAT SHOULD I READ?

Read anything and everything. It doesn't matter so much *what* you read as that you just read. Perhaps you love to sink into a chair with a favorite novel. Maybe you're working your way through a stack of magickal texts. Or, you might devour a monthly magazine, or read the morning paper with a cup of tea. Whatever your chosen materials, read every day—consider this an important part of your writer's training.

HOW SHOULD I READ?

If you really want to get the most you can out of your reading, you'll read with a pen or pencil in hand. Yes, I'm asking you to write in your books. I know, I know. . . . Mother always told you never to write in a book, that books were sacred. She was right: books *are* sacred. But she was wrong about not writing in your books. When I was a little girl, my mother made it clear that I was never, ever to make so much as a mark in books, and for years—okay, decades—I followed that rule. But then I went back to college to become a writing teacher, and one of the first things my teachers explained was the necessity for adding notes and comments to my books, right there on the pages. Here's why.

Every piece of writing has at least two kinds of meaning: the meaning the writer intended and infused into it as she wrote, and the meaning that the reader gleans from the material as he reads. This interaction between author and reader is what brings writing to life, and this is where the pen comes in: as you read, underline passages that you find important or beautiful. Make notes and ask questions in the margin. Circle unfamiliar words that you need to look up. Mark important details, symbols, and plot points. This is how you become a critical reader. And this is important, because as a student of magick, you've studied many books and gleaned important information from each of them. By reading critically and interacting with your reading, you *involve* yourself with your books and take an active role in your own discovery process.

Ask these questions as you read:

- Is this a familiar theme, or is the content new to me?

- How does the writing make me feel?

- What is the main idea?

- How are the ideas presented?

- Do I agree with the writer?

- Is there a cultural or historical link or context?

- Does the work remind me of anything?

- What is the writer's purpose?

- How does the writer make her point?

- What symbolism do I find, and what does it mean?

The fancy word for these in-text notes is textual annotation. I've found the best annotating tool to be a fine-tip ballpoint pen, which writes in small script and makes a sharp, thin line. Gel and felt-tipped pens tend to bleed through pages. Some readers like to use a bright felt-tipped highlighter, but I don't recommend these, as they tend to cover your pages with nondescript pastel islands. When you go back later and study your highlighted sections, it can be hard to tell why you highlighted the passage in the first place. Using a fine-tipped pen allows you to record specific impressions and thoughts about the passage. You can also annotate with symbols. For instance, I draw a small skeleton key in the margin next to a "key idea," sketch a sparking wand to highlight magickal practices, etc.

If you have an old, valuable, or treasured book, you might not want to write in it. In this case, "annotate" with paper bookmarks or sticky notes. If you plan to leave either in place for longer than a month, make sure they're made of acid-free materials.

Annotation is a great way to show that texts exist to be questioned, reacted to, and even argued with. By annotating as you read, you'll come to understand more about how you read and how you think; this will help you be a better reader, a better writer, and a better magick practitioner. Best of all, your margin notes may later contribute to a great story idea or a powerful magickal working. And there's nothing more exciting than opening a book and finding it full of your own notes made over the years—what a wonderful way to reflect!

BUILDING A LIBRARY

Building your own personal library is a matter of time, space, and money. You need the time to decide which books you want on your shelves, and the time to find them. Space is important—books can take up a surprising expanse, and they must be stored under reasonable conditions, i.e., in a warm, dry room and out of direct sunlight. Finally, you need money—most books aren't free. Fortunately, it's easy to find good used (I prefer to call them experienced) books in used bookstores, both online and in real space. Some organizations—like Bookcrossing (see Resources)—provide ways to swap or acquire books for free. Personal library websites—such as LibraryThing.com (see Resources)—are the newest trend on the Internet. LibraryThing guides you through cataloging and organizing your personal library, as well as linking you to others who share similar reading interests. Other home librarians experiment with different ways of organizing their collections, even creating their own computerized or hands-on card catalogues. By the way: if you loan a book to a friend, be sure to write down the book title and date on a designated page in your writing (or reading) journal.

There are many other ways to have fun with your own library. You might want to design or purchase bookplates, adhesive panels that are placed inside the book's front cover (or on an early page), and say something along the lines of, "From the Splendiferous Library of Moonwriter." Some readers have a rubber stamp or an embosser created with which to personalize their books (just make sure any ink is acid free). Or, make bookmarks: cut strips of heavy decorative paper or leather and add magickal symbols or scripts.

CREATING A READING LIFE LIST . . . AND HABIT

Just as birdwatchers create life lists of birds they've seen, you can start a life list of books you've read. Include author, title, edition, copyright date, and ISBN, plus the date you read the book and a general review of the book and your impressions. Add a category description: cosmology, divination, mystery, etc. You might even create your own rating system, e.g., "This book rates 3.5 wands." Create the list by hand or use a resource like LibraryThing.com. Your list will be fun to put together and should provide you with hours of inspiration. Your family members will appreciate it, too—imagine if you had a list of your grandmother's favorite works. Your life list could become a valuable addition to your family's archives.

It'll be easy to add to the life list, for I'm going to recommend that you read for at least thirty minutes every day, and longer if possible. Remember: a good writer must be a good reader. Consider this an essential part of your writing apprenticeship.

For best results, make it easy to indulge your reading habit. Keep a book-in-progress on the nightstand. Check out your local library for books on tape (or CDs) to listen to in the car, or download digital versions. I always keep a car book going, too—a hands-on text

*W*RITER'S
GRIMOIRE
The International Standard Book Number (ISBN) is a unique number assigned to each book as it is published. It encodes specific information about a book's publisher, country of origin, title, and more.

in the glove box for those moments when you find yourself waiting for the bank to open, standing in line at school conferences, etc.

Vary your reading as much as you can. Some people fall into a pattern of only reading nonfiction, graphic novels, magickal texts, etc. While there's nothing wrong with that, the more you can read, and the more *different* things you read, the more types of writing you'll be exposed to. For a blossoming writer, this is crucial.

 *Scribbulus* _____

1. Start your own reading life list. Include favorite books from your childhood, as well as the books that have been important to you during your lifetime.

2. Think of a magickal or mundane text that has been important to you. Reflect on why it has been so meaningful, and how it has shaped or redirected you in some way. How or when did you discover it? What is it that attracts or empowers you? Freewrite on your thoughts, or make a journal entry about them.

twelve

QUILL AND SCROLL

The study of letters and alphabets—especially those considered magickal or arcane—is a great way to engage with the craft of writing. Working with arcane alphabets will help you feel magickally connected with scribes of the past, as well as providing a powerful and enjoyable addition to your ritual and spellcraft. And if you can brings special pens, quills, and inks into the process, even better. Let's take a walk back through time. . . .

EARLY ALPHABETS

The oldest-known forms of writing came from ancient Mesopotamia, in the fertile Cradle of Civilization ("fertile crescent") between the Tigris and Euphrates rivers—land known today as Iraq. The earliest Mesopotamians—the Sumerians—developed the cuneiform alphabet about 3100 BCE. *Cuneiform* (literally "wedge-shaped") symbols were made with sharp sticks and wet clay, each symbol eventually coming to represent a discrete object, action, or idea.

Around 3000 BCE, the ancient Egyptians created a similar form of symbolic writing known as hieroglyphics. In hieroglyphic script, each *glyph* ("carving") was actually a tiny picture-image that might represent a thing, action, syllable-sound, or linking text. Hieroglyphic writing was later converted by Egypt's "New Kingdom" into a form called *hieratic*, which actually began to convert the pictorial glyphs into early abstract letters. The Egyptians further worked hieratic writing into a derived form known as *demotic* script. These early forms of writing were and are still used by magickal practitioners as a means of secret or arcane writing.

In terms of early writing systems, the first true alphabet was probably the Hebrew alphabet, which Moses received directly from YHWH, the Hebrew god, around 1628 BCE. An alphabet is a set of symbols or letters that exists in a fixed order and is used to represent the basic sounds of a spoken language. Most historic and modern alphabets include thirty or fewer letters; the Hebrew alphabet contains twenty-two, with five letters taking a different form when ending a word. Another progenitor of early alphabets came from Phoenicia, an ancient nation on the shores of the eastern Mediterranean Sea, corresponding to modern Lebanon and the coastal plains of Syria.

Phoenicia consisted of a number of city-states and was a flourishing center of Mediterranean trade and colonization during the early part of the first millennium BCE. The Phoenician alphabet became the ancestor of the Greek and Roman alphabets. Around 1000–900 BCE, the ancient Greeks used written Phoenician to create the first modern alphabet, named for a combination of the alphabet's first two letters: *alpha + beta*. The Greek alphabet—the first to include both vowel and consonant sounds—developed in two branches: Etruscan and Cyrillic. Around 50 BCE, invading Romans usurped and conquered the Greek civilization; over time, the Romans further modified the Etruscan alphabet into a written Roman alphabet for writing Latin. That Etrusco-Roman alphabet is essentially what we use today, while the Greek Cyrillic alphabet evolved into the written language of Russian.

The world of legend and myth is filled with tales of mythic and magickal languages. The Futhark (FOO-thark) or "runic" alphabet— named for its first six letters: f, u, th, a (or o), r, and k—is probably the best known of the ancient, arcane writing systems. According to legend, runic letters were a gift of a Norse goddess, Mother Idun, keeper of the Norse gods' magic apples of immortality. Mother Idun engraved the runic letters on the tongue of her consort, Bragi, allowing him to learn their meanings and making him into the first great poet. The Norse god Odin—thought to perhaps be a masculinized version of Idun—acquired his own knowledge of the runes through sacrifice: he hung himself from the World Tree for nine days and nights. As he neared death, he was gifted with a vision of runic symbols. He escaped with his life, but gave up the sight in one eye in return for the gift of the runes. In a neat meshing of reality and myth, runic writings have been found throughout northern Europe; most date to the early Gothic period, c. 1000 CE, but the earliest-known full set of twenty-four runes dates to 400 CE, found on the Kylver Stone in Gotland, a Swedish island-province.

The Theban alphabet is another medieval writing system that may have been created as a means to encode Latin. It is sometimes called Honorarian, in honor of its supposed creator, Honorious III (var. "Honorius the Theban"), who probably authored the medieval magick text *Liber Juratus* (the "Sworn Book of Honorios"). Theban is widely used today by modern magickal practitioners and is sometimes referred to as "The Witch's Alphabet." The early Celts used the Ogham or "tree alphabet," a simple system of short lines and slash marks carved into sticks or rock; it can still be used for communication and works well as a divination system. Pictish is a writing system (not a true alphabet) based on the Ogham-driven symbols used by the Picts of the ancient British Isles. Raymond Buckland adopted this system and added his own conventions for use in Pecti-Wita, a Scottish tradition.

Other magickal alphabets—including Hermetic fonts (such as Coptic, Enochian, or Pass of the River) were used most often by ceremonial religions and by highly trained priests and magi, many of whom were required to study for years before the mysteries of their tradition's alphabets were revealed to them as an important rite of passage.

You can examine some magickal alphabets in the appendix.

MAGICKAL SCRIPTS

In many traditions, letters and alphabets themselves are magickal. The ancient Greeks believed that the world was created when the Greek vowels were spoken aloud. Likewise, Jews were taught that the Hebrew letters were responsible for creating life. Arabic, Hebrew, Chinese, and ancient Greek scripts were seen as possessing their own inherent powers. Many modern traditions involve studying and meditating on the meaning of specific alphabet systems or individual letters, including the Phoenician and Ogham alphabets and the Greater Futhark Runes.

MAGICKAL MENTION

The Ogham—pronounced OH-umm or OH-gum—is an ancient Celtic alphabet that uses sequences of parallel lines cut into twigs. Ogham served as both a writing system and a divinatory tool.

Sigils, Glyphs, and Acronyms

Taken from the Latin *sigillum*, or "sign," a sigil is an inscribed, drawn, or painted symbol considered to possess magickal power. Many magickal traditions use sigils, including those of the Romany, Haitian Vodoun, Candomble, Rangoli (India), Pemba (Brazil), and Pennsylvania Dutch Pow Wow practice. Modern magick practitioners combine runic characters or arcane alphabets to create sigils.

The word *glyph* comes from the French *glyphe*, literally a carved or inscribed pictograph—a sculpted picture. As discussed earlier, hieroglyphic script was a picture-alphabet used in ancient Egyptian and other writing systems.

While sigils are usually charged and considered to carry an individual's magickal power or strength, glyphs serve more as a tool of communication. Glyphs may also be drawn in the air or incised into the ground (or other solid materials) to invite or honor a desired spirit.

An acronym is a word formed from the initial letters of other words. For example, LASER is an acronym for "light amplification

*M*AGICKAL
MENTION
The "Sacred Alphabet" or "Alphabet of Desire" refers to a system of cards and sigils created by Austin Osman Spare in the early 1900s and aimed at expressing desire. The philosophical background to this system is explained in Spare's book, *The Book of Pleasure*. Spare's work with sigils played an important role in the development of modern chaos magicks.

by stimulated emission of radiation." You can harness the mystery of the acronym by creating your own. Your magickal journal might be named with an acronym, the meaning of which only you know. Or, you might use an acronym in spellwork—for example, you could recite the word *power* to direct energy during ritual, knowing that the acronym meant "Proceed Outward With Eternal Radiance."

WRITERS' TOOLS THROUGH THE AGES

The Quill

Quills are among the oldest-known writing instruments. They're usually made from the feathers of large birds—geese, turkeys, etc.—and are known for their flexibility and their ability to inscribe a fine, sharp line. Before quills, humans used sharpened reeds to write on papyrus—a practice that probably dates back to the ancient Egyptians and Neolithic times. Quills eventually replaced reeds and were used well into the nineteenth century.

Make Your Own Quill

To make a writing quill, start with a found bird feather or a large quill from the craft store. Remove most of the feather, leaving just a tuft on the end. Use a pocketknife to cut the quill's sharp end into a broad, flat surface, then use the quill—dipped in ink—like a calligraphy pen. Quills are fun to work with, but the tips wear out quickly. If the quill

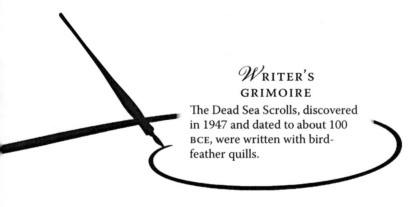

$\mathcal{W}$RITER'S
GRIMOIRE
The Dead Sea Scrolls, discovered in 1947 and dated to about 100 BCE, were written with bird-feather quills.

is long enough, a worn or broken tip can be cut off and the quill sharpened to a new point. Eventually, when the feather gets too short, you'll have to toss it out. A variation is to use superglue to attach a calligraphy nib to the end of a feather or quill. Twigs and reeds can also be carved into quick writing tools, with the magick of the wood itself increasing the power of the writing.

The Pencil

The first pencil was probably a chunk of charcoal or a burnt twig, but the pencil as we know it is credited to the Romans, who used lead styluses to write on papyrus sheets. Pencils evolved into wooden cylinders wrapped around a lead core. In the sixteenth century, the discovery of graphite deposits saw graphite became the main component of pencils, with the first models consisting of a piece of sheepskin or leather bound tightly around a stick of graphite. The Italians came up with the idea of putting a wooden case around a graphite core. Modern pencil lead is actually a mixture of powdered graphite pigment and a clay binder. The materials are kiln-fired to form the pencil cores we know today; the more clay used in the mixture, the harder the pencil lead.

Pencils are graded according to a European system that describes them in terms of hardness (H) and blackness (B). On one end of the spectrum is the 9H, which has extremely hard lead and draws a

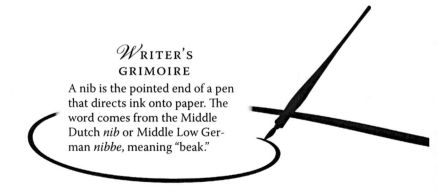

𝒲RITER'S GRIMOIRE
A nib is the pointed end of a pen that directs ink onto paper. The word comes from the Middle Dutch *nib* or Middle Low German *nibbe*, meaning "beak."

sharp, fine line. On the other end is the 9B, which has soft, charcoal-like lead and draws a soft, indistinct line that smudges easily. The standard writing pencil is known as HB and falls in the center of the range. The HB system is used worldwide, particularly by artists. A second system, adopted in the United States by Henry David Thoreau, rates pencils on a hardness scale from #1 to #4; on this scale, our standard writing tool is the well-known #2 pencil.

Most pencils today contain the standard graphite/clay core, but other common types of pencils include those made of charcoal, pastels, or a colored graphite pigment. China markers are grease pencils that write on any surface. Watercolor pencils have a water-soluble pigment, allowing the pencil markings to be shaped and washed with brush and water. A pencil's shape can be distinct, too. For example, carpenters use thick, flat pencils that won't roll off the workbench and are strong enough to write on wood without snapping.

Pencils may be sharpened with a small hand-held sharpener, a piece of sandpaper, or a sharp pocketknife. HB, 2B, and 3B leads hold a point well and need little sharpening, while softer leads don't hold a point at all but are excellent for shading when laid on their sides.

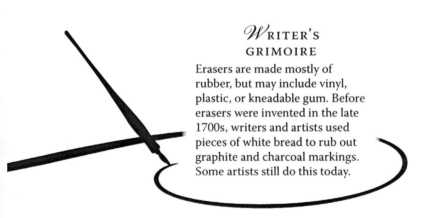

*W*RITER'S GRIMOIRE

Erasers are made mostly of rubber, but may include vinyl, plastic, or kneadable gum. Before erasers were invented in the late 1700s, writers and artists used pieces of white bread to rub out graphite and charcoal markings. Some artists still do this today.

The Pen

The pen is a writing instrument that holds ink, directs the ink into a writing surface, and provides a point for writing with the ink. Every pen is an offspring of the quill. What we know as a pen first began around 100 CE, when metal nibs were fastened onto sticks, reeds, or bird-feather quills and used with ink and inkwells. The fountain pen came next, providing the ability to write long texts without having to dip repeatedly into an inkwell. Ballpoint pens came into wide use in the early twentieth century, and felt tips and rollerball tips arrived in the mid- to late 1900s.

Many magickal writers reserve and dedicate a special pen and ink for important magickal purposes. This could be anything from a simple ballpoint pen to an elaborate fountain pen or fine writing instrument made of wood, resin, metal, or even blown glass. What makes the pen special isn't so much what it looks like as how it is consecrated and used. Consider, also, that pen and inkwell can serve as a writer's metaphoric stand-ins for male and female correspondences in ritual or spellwork—e.g., the athame and the cauldron, the chalice and the blade.

*M*AGICKAL
MENTION

Dedicate a special pen for use in your Books of Shadows or for other "most magickal" purposes. Bless and consecrate this tool: perhaps you'll call it your "magick quill," "Pen of Words," or "Pen of Authority." When not in use, wrap your magick pen in a special cloth and store in a decorated box or other protected place.

When sketching in a magickal journal or working with illumination (see Chapter 13), I suggest using a fine-tip black felt pen. These draw crisp lines that look sharp whether left unadorned or embellished with color. Look for a pen that has permanent ink and won't bleed through your paper. You won't be able to erase your mistakes, so you might choose to do the initial work in pencil, and then trace over it with the permanent ink.

The Ink

Because of their abilities to transform thoughts into symbols and words, inks were regarded by the ancients as magickal tools in an of themselves, and one of the first jobs—upon acquiring or creating a new ink—was to purify it.

The first, simplest inks were likely made by dissolving bits of ash, soot, lampblack, or powdered minerals in water and straining away the lumps. Other early inks used ground metals, squid ink, and various plant saps and berries. Eventually people realized that substances could affect the color, consistency, and permanence of the mixture. Today's inks are complex mixtures varying from the thin ink used in calligraphy to the more viscous inks used in commercial printing.

Magickal Ink

Most magick and New Age stores sell an array of magick inks—most of which are simply plain old stationery store inks with fancy names like "Dragon's Blood" or "Dove's Blood." You may enjoy the esoteric aspects they add to your *sanctum sanctorum*. Actual ink making requires the mixing of several substances:

- *A base solvent*: Usually isopropyl alcohol (available at your local pharmacy). Water may also be used—especially infused (e.g., rose water) or charged (e.g., moon water) waters.

White vinegar and hydrogen peroxide are sometimes used as solvents.

- *Pigment*: Usually a base of high-quality ink in a desired color (available at office and stationery stores) or various forms of carbon, such a soot, lampblack, or charcoal. Saffron threads (from grocer or herbalist) create a yellow-gold color. Chinese block inks—red, black, or blue—can be mixed with water or shaved into an ink mixture.

- *Resin*: Added sparingly in powdered form, to instill a mixture with a specific essence. For example, any ink labeled as "Dragon's Blood" likely includes Dragon's Blood resin.

- *Thickener*: Gum arabica (from the pharmacy) is the most common; gum tragacanth is another. Allowing ink to sit in a dish and partially evaporate over a day or two will concentrate its essence and thicken it.

- *Oil*: Like resins, these are added sparingly (one drop at a time) to infuse the ink mixture with scents and/or magickal attributes. Use with care—too much and the ink will be oily and may seep through paper or leave a stain.

*W*RITER'S GRIMOIRE

Soot or lampblack is the black material that collects when you hold an empty can or a spoon over a flame. The sooty residue can be scraped off and collected for addition to an ink mixture. Vary the nature of the soot by burning different candles, wood, herbs, etc.

- *Magickal items*: During the making process, magickal items—a spell written on a small scroll, herbs, a stone or crystal, etc.—may also be steeped in the ink as a part of charging it with specific magicks or correspondences. An arcane practice suggested adding infused wormwood to ink to protect against mice and vermin. A prick of one's own blood adds power and imbues the mixture with the user's purposes.

As you can infer from the above, ink making is a complex process. But it's also lots of fun. If you want to give it a try, work with non-reactive containers (use plastic, glass, or steel; avoid copper, aluminum, and iron) and wooden or steel utensils. Measure ingredients carefully and write down every step, so that you can revise the recipe as needed.

Experimenting with thickness is one of the trickiest parts of the ink-making process. If using a fountain pen, the ink needs to be quite liquid so that it can flow through the pen's mechanism. If writing with a traditional quill, the ink must be thick enough to cling to the quill. Always filter your finished ink through cheese-

*W*RITER'S GRIMOIRE

What we call India ink is a deep-black, permanent ink containing dispersed carbon particles. Indian ink dates back to the seventeenth century, where it originally referred to Chinese and Japanese pigment inks prepared in solid blocks and imported to Europe via India. India ink is widely used today by artists and calligraphers.

cloth or unbleached cotton before using. Store in a tightly capped glass bottle or inkwell, out of direct light.

Moonwriting Ink: A Recipe. Here's one recipe you might enjoy trying. It's made from easy to find, nontoxic ingredients, and you'll feel like a medieval chemist as you brew it up.

> **Moonwriting Ink**
> 1 black tea bag
> ⅓ c. charged full moon water
> A small saucepan
> ¼ c. white vinegar
> 1 unsoaped steel wool pad
> Small bowl
> Unbleached cotton/cheesecloth
> Toothpick or wooden skewer
> Optional: gum arabica; 3% hydrogen peroxide (both available at drug stores)

Place the tea bag in a teacup. Bring the full moon water to a boil; pour it over the tea bag and let steep for 15 minutes. Wring tea bag out and throw away. The tea now contains tannic acid.

In a small saucepan, warm the vinegar. Use scissors to snip bits of unsoaped steel wool into the hot vinegar, making sure the vinegar covers the steel wool. Heat until the steel wool dissolves and/or forms a colored solution (iron sulfate). Allow to cool.

Pour the tea into the small bowl. Use a piece of unbleached cotton to strain the iron solution into the tea. This will form black iron tannate. Be very careful: this is indelible and will stain whatever it touches.

Dip a toothpick or skewer into the "ink" and try writing with it. If it's too thick, thin the ink with a few drops of hydrogen peroxide. If the ink seems watery, let it sit out for a day or two until enough evaporates to make it slightly thicker. Alternately, add dabs of gum arabica to thicken the mixture.

Invisible Inks. Invisible inks have two qualities: one, they're either invisible when applied or become invisible soon after; and two, they can later be made visible, allowing the original message to be read. Most invisible inks work by light, heat, or chemical reactions.

With heat-based invisible inks, the message is allowed to dry and is then retrieved by heating the paper, e.g., holding it over an incandescent light bulb, ironing it, etc. Examples of these inks include cola drinks, lemon juice, milk, vinegar, and white wine.

Chemical-acting invisible inks use acid-base reactions to cause dried ink to change color and become visible. An ink of liquid laundry starch or lemon juice can be revealed with an application of diluted iodine.

$\mathscr{M}$AGICKAL MENTION

While ink is a useful means of constructing magick, it can also be an important part of banishing or releasing spells and charms. You'll need a bowl of water, paper, quill, and water-soluble ink. Use the ink to write the words that you wish to banish or release. As part of the spellwork or ritual, dip the paper into the water, and watch as the words slip away and vanish. Green magick practitioners might prefer to do this beside a river or lake, or even at ocean's edge.

A Simple Disappearing Ink Recipe
4 drops lemon juice
4 drops onion juice (from a grated onion)
17 grains of granulated sugar

Mix the above ingredients in a large spoon. Dip a toothpick into the mixture and write messages on white paper. To read the messages hold the paper over a warm light bulb.

Light-based invisible inks are those that glow when exposed to ultraviolet or black light. Special fluorescent inks may be purchased for this purpose. Laundry detergents that contain "brighteners" can be mixed with water to create a light-based invisible ink.

Invisible inks have many magickal applications. You might use these inks to record or transmit messages in secrecy. Or you could use them to inscribe runes or symbols of protection on magickal tools or objects. Note: you may need to dilute the ink as needed with water to make your message vanish thoroughly as it dries.

Invisible ink could be used as part of a spell of unveiling or discovery. Use the ink to write your desired magickal outcome on a piece of paper or scroll. Design a simple spell or ritual in which the inscribed paper is the central focus. After the working is complete, tuck the paper and its message away for safekeeping, until the spell works and the goal is realized. Then, use a revealer to uncover the original writing. With the outcome realized, offer thanks, and dispose of the paper by burying or burning.

Inkwells

Inkwells of glass, crystal, stone, ceramic, and even wood provide a storage place for your inks and add pizzazz to the shelves of your *sanctum*. The ancient *Grimorium Verum* (an Egyptian tome dating to the sixteenth century) recommended that a magician's ink bottles and inkwell be inscribed with the following Hebrew script, believed to send divine power into the ink and to ward off evil powers and influences:*

YOD HE VAV HE

METATRON

YAD

KADOSH

ELOYM

SABAOTH

Scroll and Papermaking

Magickal journals and Books of Shadows require paper, and many spells and rituals are written down as well. Paper has a long, romantic history. Before anything akin to paper was invented, Stone Age writers wrote on stone, wood, pottery shards, or even in the mud. Later, writing shifted to papyrus, parchment, and vellum.

Papyrus

An early paper made from layered and pounded stems of the papyrus plant, papyrus was first used in ancient Egypt between 3000 and 800 BCE. Papyrus use spread into western Asia and was widely used until the coming of paper.

Parchment

Named for the city Pergamon (where it was invented), parchment is made from the skin of a calf, sheep, or goat and was used by medieval bookmakers for its durability. Today, replica parchment is used for diplomas and other important documents.

---

*Illes, *The Element Encyclopedia of 5000 Spells,* 1062.

Vellum

A fine grade of parchment made originally from the skin of a calf. The classical grimoires were often written on parchment or vellum to enhance the text's worth and durability. Today's craft store "vellum" is a stiff, plastic-based, semi-transparent material, completely unrelated to the animal-based original.

Paper

Invented in China during the first century CE, paper was prepared in thin sheets from wood pulp or other fibrous substances (e.g., hemp).

Today's craft stores are stocked with paper in every imaginable texture, color, and pattern, as well as with kits for papermaking. Papermaking lets you control the components and essences that go into the paper. You may want to make your own paper for important spells in which paper plays a central role or is used as a tool. For instance, you could imbue a special paper recipe with essential oils, botanicals, fragrance, or moon- or crystal-charged water.

You might also work with textured or colored papers, depending on your intention:

- A piece of sandpaper could make an appropriate altar "cloth" for a ritual oriented toward the earth element.

- A piece of brown paper bag could create a rustic-appearing paper for arcane purposes, especially if you tear and then burn the edges.

- A piece of gold paper could be used for a spell involving abundance, white paper for cleansing, etc.

- Modern "parchment" paper from the craft store makes an attractive scroll.

- Certain tree barks may be used for more authentic scrolls. Use only "found" or shed bark; never strip bark from a living tree.

Sycamore is a good choice for this: it sheds its bark naturally, and is associated with creativity and insight.

To make your own free-form scrolls, wrap a piece of parchment tightly around a dowel or wooden spoon handle. Tie with a ribbon and allow to sit for a few days to help the shape "take." Slip the scroll off the dowel; it's ready for use, and should be stored rolled and tied closed. For a more traditional scroll, glue one or both ends of the paper to dowels (choose and adorn the wood as appropriate to your purposes), roll, and proceed as above.

Paper as Magickal Item

When a spell is inscribed on a piece of paper, and particularly if the spell is spoken aloud at the same time, the paper becomes a working part of the magickal action. Paper charms may be carried in the pocket, hung above a door or threshold, pasted inside a Book of Shadows, or used in a myriad of other ways. Some must be altered or even destroyed—by burning, burying, etc.—in order to release their effects. A spell written on a paper airplane can be cast into the wind, while a paper boat or spell-in-a-bottle can sail away on a stream. (Just be sure not to litter!) Strips of paper infused with intention and crafted into links in a paper chain may be used to "count down" or mark timed events, with links removed at the appropriate time. You can even buy rice paper that dissolves in the mouth: the perfect adjunct to a working of kitchen magick.

Paper and writing can also become a kind of talisman; certificates of apprenticeship, diplomas, handfasting certificates, etc., are magickal talismans, exerting a lasting type of protection or guardianship—especially when hung on the wall in a position of power.

The effect is enhanced by the color and nature of the paper and ink used, and by the presence of signatures, sigils, and symbols.

Writing without Paper

Magickal writing need not always involve paper. Consider these options:

- Write or cast a spell into the air, with finger or wand inscribing the magickal words and sending them into the sky (especially effective for spells invoking the air element or the celestial realm).

- Trace words in the mud and allow to weather away naturally. (Good for earth element spells, or those in which the caster wants to gain freedom from something.)

- Trace words in wet sand above the surf line at low tide; the incoming seas will wash the sand clean and smooth. (Good for water spells, or for referencing a clean slate.)

*M*AGICKAL
MENTION

No discussion of "paper magick" could be complete without mentioning flash paper. This paper is designed to burn up, well . . . in a flash! Write a spell on it, ignite it, and POOF, it'll go up in smoke. Flash paper is especially effective in group work or ritual, and is a terrific way to work with the element of fire. Purchase flash paper at magic or New Age shops.

- Write words on a piece of wood and burn in a ritual fire. (Excellent for fire element workings, or for a metaphor of rebirth.)

- Paint or inscribe a spell on a piece of pottery or ceramic, and then shatter it, releasing the energy.

- Create words on a sidewalk or the ground by strewing birdseed, salt, cornmeal, granular plant food, sand, flour, or some other natural ingredient and allowing it to be dispersed by the elements. (Sand paintings and mandalas are variations on this theme.)

- Build words from pebbles or small stones and leave in place until removed by the caster or naturally dispersed.

- Carve a spell onto a piece of food—e.g., an apple—with a toothpick and then eat the food, allowing the spell's energy to enter your body.

- Carve a spell onto a bar of soap, and use for ritual cleansing—either to imbue the bather with the spell's essence or to wash away unwanted energies.

- Dip a finger in honey and write "honeyed words" inside a cup or glass, which can then be filled with a beverage and consumed. (Perfect for love spells!)

Those are only a few approaches—use your imagination to create others. Anything that you can write *on* can be used as a writing surface, and anything that you can write *with* can become a "pen." Colored chalks are wonderful for writing on sidewalks and driveways, and they wash away with the rain. Special window pens (purchase at a craft shop) allow one to write on windows and mirrors, with easy cleanup.

Sealing Wax

Sealing wax is both fun and practical: it not only signs or endorses your magickal workings, but helps secure them from prying eyes. Sealing wax comes as a dense, narrow stick of colored wax with a wick; the wick is lit, and melted wax is dripped into a pool on the letter or envelope, after which a small metal stamp is used to emboss an image into the still-soft wax. The stamps come in an array of initials, magickal symbols, and astrological glyphs. The wax seal becomes part of your signature, or—if placed across an envelope's gummed flap—helps increase security, as anyone who opens the envelope will also break the seal. In Roman times, military rulers wore signet rings that were used to stamp and authenticate wax seals.

 *Scribbulus* _____

1. Make magickal ink. Use one of the methods in this chapter, or for an ultra-simple ink, crush ¼ c. frozen raspberries, strain the juice, and thicken with a few drops of honey or corn syrup. (Note: use this "ink" only with a quill: don't load this into your favorite fountain pen as it's likely to gum the works!) This ink is lovely on heavy, parchment-type paper, and infuses your writings with the fruit's magickal colors and attributes.

2. Work with magickal alphabets and symbols to create your own magickal sigil. Even the Roman alphabet can create terrific effects when the letters are rotated, superimposed on one another, etc.

3. Create a piece of writing in which you use paper, ink, or color to support the writing's intention or meaning. For example, a piece of deep-blue paper and a metallic silver ink would be lovely for inscribing a lunar charm, while green ink on pale-pink or yellow paper might suit workings done during the first days of spring.

thirteen

Make Your Writing Beautiful

Writing and journaling are satisfying by themselves, especially once you've created your own writing routine and settled into it. But the time might come when you watch your pen glide across the page and feel the urge to add something new. Color perhaps. Maybe a crisply lined border, a calligraphic font, or a quick sketch.

What you're feeling isn't unusual—those who work with pen and paper have long been moved to adorn their work, elevating their words to another level. Medieval Books of Hours and illuminated manuscripts were highly ornamented with brilliant inks, intricate lettering, illustrations, and even precious metals. This tradition continues with magickal grimoires and Books of Shadows, which are likewise "decorated" with colors, textures, and personal additions.

USING ARTIST'S MEDIA

While much can be done with pen and pencil alone (see Chapter 12 for more details), you might also like to experiment with traditional artist's materials in your work, especially in journals or Books of Shadows where illustrations play a big role.

Charcoal is one of the oldest drawing instruments, dating back to the first Stone Age human to notice that a piece of charcoal could make marks on stone. Today, artist's charcoal is actually carbonized wood made by kiln-firing pieces of willow, birch, vine, or other woods in airtight containers. Charcoal is wonderful to work with, and is ideal for moody, textured work. Its only real drawback is its smudginess; if you use charcoal for sketching or journaling, you'll want to use a spray fixative to set the finished work.

Chalk is made by mixing calcium carbonate with pigments. Chalk is great to work with for outdoor magick and ritual. I keep a box of classroom chalk in my magickal kit; with it, I can outline ritual space on a concrete surface or chalk directional markings on trees and stones. The chalk marks are temporary—and organic—and wear off quickly when exposed to weather.

Homemade Chalk
6–8 white eggshells
1 T. flour
1 T. lukewarm water
⅛ t. white glue

Wash eggshells and dry well. Grind to a powder with a mortar and pestle.

Mix flour and water in a small dish, forming a paste.

Stir in 1 T. of the powdered eggshell and glue. Mix well. If you want colored chalk, stir in some tempera powder.

Shape the mixture into a chubby stick and wrap in waxed paper. Let dry for at least 3 days—unroll the waxed paper as the stick begins to dry.

Use your chalk for amazing magickal purposes!

Pastels are made by mixing ground pigment, ground chalk, and a binder, such as gum arabica. The higher the proportion of binder to chalk, the harder the stick: softer pastels feel almost like drawing with a lipstick, while the hardest ones work like a stick of chalk. Like chalk and charcoal, pastels wear and smudge easily, and lasting designs need protection with fixatives.

Crayons combine a waxy base with pigments and sometimes with minerals or mineral oxides. For many of us, the whiff of a box of crayons transports us back to a moment in our childhood. Even today—and I am long past my childhood—I often buy a new box of crayons during the fall school shopping season, recycling the previous year's box in candle craft or fire starters.

Colored pencils are a simple and satisfying way to add color to your writing projects. For best results, use thick-leaded colored pencils; these have deeper color and a waxy texture, making them more effective than thin-leaded varieties. Colored pencil works best when used to fill in a pen and ink drawing rather than a sketch made with pencil, because the lead and colored pencils can become smudged and blur together. Mix and layer colors to create unique shades and special effects. Special watercolor pencils are used just

*M*AGICKAL
MENTION

Chalk is a soft white limestone (calcium carbonate) formed from the shells, bones, reefs, and fossilized remains of undersea animals. Limestone corresponds with strength, durability, connectivity, and the spirits of ancestral guardians. Use chalk in spell work linked to the water element, or in which you wish to connect yourself to your ancestors or the departed ones.

like regular colored pencils, but once the color is laid down, a fine brush can be used to lightly brush the penciled areas with water, creating a watercolor wash effect.

Watercolor paint combines pigment with a water-soluble binder, such as gum arabica. The paint is applied with soft brushes, often using water to create effects through dilutions and washings. Watercolors tend to be transparent, and light reflects from the paper's surface and through the paint, creating a luminous effect. Tempera paint is simply paint to which a binding medium has been added. Egg yolk is a traditional tempera additive. Those who like to work with tempera appreciate its thick texture and vivid colors. Acrylic paint combines pigment and synthetic resins, making it a quick-drying paint that can be applied to just about any surface. You can use acrylic paints on paper, to decorate a journal cover, or even to touch up the lamp on your writing desk.

Just about any kind of paint applied to paper can cause the paper to pucker or buckle, and "loose" paints—like watercolors—can soak through paper as well. I usually paint on a fresh sheet of paper that's separate from my notebook. Once the painting is dry, I cut it to fit and then use an acid-free glue stick to add it to my Book of Shadows, nature journal, etc.

Colored inks are also satisfying to work with. Most stationery and office supply stores sell sets of gel pens in arrays of colors, including sets of bolds, pastels, and even metallics. Rulers, plastic stencils, and French curves will help you add textual elements and borders to your work. A hard plastic carrying case or a soft roll-up leather case keeps your "adorning" tools organized and accessible.

If you enjoy lunar magick, you might try silverpoint. In this technique, silver wire (in a holder) is used on special paper. The line is silver at first, but later oxidizes (tarnishes) to a rusty brown. Silverpoint was a favorite technique of Leonardo da Vinci in the fifteenth century. For solar-oriented magick, or that associated with wealth, consider working with gold foils or gold leaf, finely beaten sheets of nearly pure gold that are applied to paper and burnished with a smooth stone (agate is traditional).

SKETCHING AND SCRAPBOOKING

Sketching can be a useful skill, allowing you to add sketches, diagrams, maps, and more to your written projects. Covering the basics of drawing is beyond the scope of this text; if you're interested in learning to draw and sketch, I'd suggest that you take a class, buy a good instructional book, or seek out a tutor. In the meantime, you can have fun practicing on your own. Work with an assortment of drawing pencils and a good sketchpad—the rough textured papers in sketchpads are specially made to work with drawing instruments.

Scrapbooking describes the practice of combining a traditional scrapbook with writing and the use of decorative papers, stickers, collage materials, and other page elements to create something akin to a multimedia experience. Scrapbooking techniques can be used to create gorgeous Books of Shadows, personal journals, and more.

CALLIGRAPHY AND MANUSCRIPT ILLUMINATION

Calligraphy (from the Greek "beauty" + "writing") is the art of decorative writing. Most calligraphy fonts appear as ornamented cursive or italicized writing. Requiring years to master, calligraphy is both art and craft. It has traditional roots in many cultures, including Japan, China, East India, Tibet, and the Middle East. A particular style of calligraphy is described as "a hand."

Calligraphy requires the use of a special pen; this is actually a penholder with a detachable metal nib. The nib has two functions: it traps and holds a small amount of ink to use in the writing, and it provides a chiseled point or tip with which to write. Many different types of nibs—copperplate, round-hand, and speedball, for example—allow writers to create different effects. Some calligraphers use flat-edged brushes of fine animal hair to draw their letters and characters. Calligraphy may involve different types and colors of ink and virtually any kind of paper.

In an illuminated manuscript, the text is supplemented by the addition of colorful ornamentation, such as decorated initials, intricate borders, or highly detailed drawings. Motifs used in illumination typically reflect heraldic or religious symbolism. When creating illuminated manuscripts, medieval scribes began by first writing the text, usually on sheets of vellum with ink and sharpened quill. Once the text was in place, decorative ornaments were added. As might be expected, manuscript illumination was expensive and time-consuming, and was thus limited to very special or important texts. Probably the most famous illuminated manuscript is *The Book of Kells*, a religious manuscript that dates to 800 CE and today resides in the Trinity College Library in Dublin, Ireland. Books of Hours, which included prayers for different times of the day as well as marking seasonal and religious celebrations, were also frequently illuminated, or at least heavily illustrated.

It's possible to buy "how to" books and kits that teach the basics of manuscript illumination and/or calligraphy. If you're lucky enough to have a Society of Creative Anachronism chapter nearby, you may find teachers and craftsmen through them.

USING ARCHIVAL MATERIALS AND TECHNIQUES

Assuming that you'd like everything you write to be around for a long, long time—decades, at least—make sure that your work is written or printed using archival, acid-free materials. Archival materials are easy to find online, as well as in stationery, office supply, and scrapbooking stores. They're clearly labeled as "archival" and/ or "acid-free."

_____

1. Working with calligraphy or a magickal alphabet, write your magickal name or a simple phrase until you can craft it from memory.

2. Using a piece of parchment-type paper, sketch a simple diagram of your altar or writing space. Indicate the four compass directions (the moon and sun rise in the east and set in the west). Add a border of some kind—perhaps in a special design or with vivid colors—and maybe a small sketch detail or two. Add this "illuminated map" to your magickal journal.

3. Take a field trip to an art supply or craft store and explore the world of papers, inks, scrapbooking supplies, and art materials. Purchase one item that's new to you, and use it in a new way in your writing, magick, journaling, or other activities.

fourteen

Making Time

As a student of magick, you didn't jump into the craft and suddenly become proficient overnight—you studied and practiced, and then studied and practiced some more. Even so, you probably felt as if you'd only begun to learn. The same is true of writing. You're working your way through this book, but your education as a writer is just beginning. You've embarked on your own writing apprenticeship. In medieval times, when craft guilds reached the height of their form, apprenticeships allowed a novice to learn a craft or trade from a master, and apprenticeships lasted five to ten years. Once an apprenticeship was completed, the new "journeyman" left his master and ventured into the realm to ply his craft. As he met other journeymen and worked in new shops and at new tasks, his skills increased. Eventually, he might become a master and take on his own students.

Your writing education is very much like this—you immerse yourself in an array of experiences designed to teach you more about the craft. With every freewrite, every story, every ritual, every draft, every spell, and every creation . . . you'll keep learning.

> *Familiarity sparks practice,*
> *Practice engenders skill,*
> *Skill creates craft,*
> *Craft inspires art.*

KEEP WRITING

The most important thing you can do as a developing writer is to write *every day*. Make yourself a writing appointment and work it into your schedule. Don't hex yourself if you miss a day here and there, but understand that the more you practice, the better you'll get. Begin your sessions with freewriting, then move on to craft a new piece or revise an existing one.

Be impervious to interruptions during your writing time—turn the cell phone off and ask the family not to knock on the door. Leave the house if you need to. Reward yourself for reaching objectives, e.g., a certain number of words or pages completed. Take yourself out to lunch, buy a new book, or indulge in some sort of treat.

EXPLORE!

Beyond your own solo practice, you might join or start a writing group. If you start a group from scratch, determine how many people you'll accept into the group, and what level of writer (from novice to expert) you'll accept. Set up a system for trading manuscripts and giving each other feedback—this can be invaluable. Go slowly, perhaps meeting monthly at first.

Many cities have writing clubs that meet at intervals and put on annual seminars or conventions. Local community centers, high schools, and colleges offer a range of writing classes and degree programs. Online writing classes are becoming more popular, as are low-residency writing programs—with most of the work done at home and occasional forays to the campus for one to two weeks of intense class work.

Writing retreats (try Googling the phrase—you'll get hundreds of hits) are available all over the world. Some work like hotels: you pay to rent a private writing space. Others are merit-based: you submit a writing sample and *vitae*, and if you're lucky enough to be selected, you win time at the retreat, often at no charge.

If you're looking for new ways to stretch your writerly self, consider putting together a family, coven, or circle newsletter. Develop a fresh magickal journal or Book of Shadows. Start a magickal blog, write a zine, write and record a podcast, or put together a spiritual website. The more you explore your opportunities to write, the better your writing will become.

You might consider entering writing contests (again, search Google). Before entering a contest, do your homework, finding out as much as you can about what they're looking for and what past winners' entries looked like. Submit your best work, carefully proofread.

Travel is essential for writers. When you travel to a different place you meet new people, eat unfamiliar foods, and see different sights, providing fresh material for your craft. When you take part in different magickal events and rituals, you likewise experience magick in new ways, seen through fresh eyes. Keep a notepad in hand and record

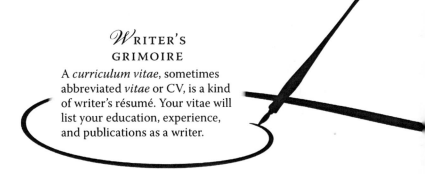

$\mathcal{W}$RITER'S GRIMOIRE

A *curriculum vitae*, sometimes abbreviated *vitae* or CV, is a kind of writer's résumé. Your vitae will list your education, experience, and publications as a writer.

details, conversations, and insights. Sketch maps and take photos—these will help you reconstruct details later on.

LISTEN TO OTHER WRITERS

Most communities host readings by writers and poets—these are often associated with libraries or bookstores. Don't miss the opportunity to see and hear your favorite writers in action. There's something special about hearing the words of prose or poetry read aloud by the person who created them. In many cases, you can also meet and talk to the reader after the event—you might even be able to have a copy of the author's book signed.

SUBMIT

As a self-styled apprentice, your first goal is to practice and hone your craft. But eventually, you'll probably be interested in getting something published. Making this transition is both exciting and scary, and there's only one way to do it: start submitting your work.

The good news is that there's a thriving "for-pay" magickal market just waiting for writers to contribute essays, stories, book reviews, and more. Pay a visit to your local magickal or New Age bookstore and go through magazines to find addresses, editors' names, and submission guidelines. (Much of this information is also available on the Internet.) Look into local magickal or spiritual newsletters. A publication like *The Writer's Market* (see Resources) will point out potential markets and guide you along.

Always follow submission guidelines precisely when sending in your work. Some publishers simply ask for a completed manuscript, while others request a query letter. The point of a query letter is to pitch your idea to an editor without actually sending in the piece, giving the editor a chance to decide whether she can use your idea. Keep your query letter concise and to the point.

Once you begin sending out your work, be prepared to get rejection notices—publishers are selective and at any given time, you're more likely to have a piece rejected than accepted. Rejection notices are part of the game and practice of becoming a writer. In his wonderful book, *On Writing*, Stephen King talks about pounding a long nail into the ceiling of his attic-eave bedroom. "By the time I was fourteen the nail in my wall would no longer support the weight of the rejection slips impaled on it. I replaced the nail with a spike and went on writing."

If the rejections include any feedback, try to learn from it, but waste no time getting your next piece ready to send out. Eventually, you'll get something published. Once you've been published, you can include that information in your query letters and other communications, and it will make it easier for you to be published a second time, and a third, and so forth.

WORKING WITH WRITING SPARKS

Many writing texts and online sites give long lists of writing prompts—written cues or ideas for writers to respond to. I like to call these "Sparks," for I imagine them igniting fires deep within. Try out some of those I've listed below—they're a great way to begin any writing session. Create your own Sparks page in your writing journal, adding ideas and inspirations as they come to you.

Sabbat Sparks

For Samhain

It is the beginning of a new year, a new cycle.

In the back corner of a magick shop, you come upon an ancient, dusty cauldron of cast iron.

You host a dumb supper.

Consider the importance of memory.

You part the veils, and see _____.

You speak to a dearly departed one.

For Yule

The winter earth is spectral, cold, and silent.

Describe your most memorable display of winter lights.

You plan a feast for the Solstice.

You kindle a Yule fire.

You pass the drinking horn at a Bardic Circle.

You envision death.

For Imbolc

You spend a clear winter night stargazing.

Contemplate candle magick.

Consider your magickal talents.

Consider all things gold.

What scents do you equate with winter? Why?

Visualize a skeletal, leafless tree in the dead of winter.

For Ostara

You inscribe and bury an egg as part of your sunrise ritual.

You invite your friends to a sunrise meal, with eggs as the central dish.

You undergo an initiation.

What does rebirth mean to you?

Describe your favorite herb.

Visualize a spring tree covered with blossoms.

For Beltane

How does passion feel?

How does fertility find its place in your life?

Consider a past love.

You work a spell of power and strength.

What is red?

You dance around a balefire.

For Litha

You contemplate the longest day of the year.

You craft kitchen magick.

Consider the meaning and impact of the Wiccan Rede, or its
equivalent in your tradition.

How does green feel?

Reflect on your favorite spring salad. Describe it on paper, using as
many of the five senses as possible.

Consider summer vacation.

For Lughnasadh

You bake bread.

You brew an herbal potion.

Consider the meaning of health and well-being.

Make a list of favorite summer pastimes.

How does high summer smell? Sound? Feel?

Imagine standing in a field of tall, ripening corn.

For Mabon

You bring in the harvest.

Consider the meaning of balance in your life.

You are sitting beneath an ancient, wise tree.

Apple pies are baking in your kitchen, right now.

Write about your perfect feast meal.

Consider the meanings of elderhood.

Esbat Sparks

A full lunar eclipse hangs overhead.

It is the time of the dark moon.

You've heard about Blood Moons, Storm Moons, and Hunting
Moons. Create your own name for a full moon.

You dance skyclad under the moon.

You find meaning in the moon's markings.

You prepare for an Esbat ritual.

You draw down (or write down) the moon.

You gaze at the moon. What do you see?

You stand in a night-blooming moon garden.

Elemental Sparks

Earth Sparks

You explore a deep, unknown cave.

Consider how the earth element supports your life.

You stand atop a tall mountain.

You walk a ley line. What do you feel?

You discover a faery circle in your garden.

You circle the ring of Stonehenge.

Describe a favorite stone.

Reflect on the nature of perseverance.

You hold a beautiful crystal: the philosopher's stone.

Reflect on circles and cycles in life.

Consider the sense of touch.

Air Sparks

You call the wind, and breathe in its inspirations.

You watch a windstorm.

You fly a kite.

You hang a set of ethereal wind chimes.

Consider the sense of hearing.

You see pictures in the clouds.

You watch a rainstorm far in the distance.

You are invisible.

You trap wind in your cupped hands. What do you feel? Hear?

Fire Sparks

You ride a dragon.

Consider the most impetuous thing you've ever done.

You lay and kindle a fire.

You fire-scry.

You receive an energy attunement.

Your heart pounds. Why?

Reflect on the meaning of emotions.

Consider the sense of taste.

Imagine a brilliant red cloak.

You hold a candle that is gifted with eternal fire.

Water Sparks

Like the waters of life, you transform.

You engage in a ritual immersion.

You wash your face in the morning dew.

You scry with a basin of rainwater.

You perspire. Why?

You hold a beaker full of the waters of life.

Consider the sense of sight.

While hiking, you come upon a hidden spring of bath-warm water.

You stand in the rain until you are soaked.

Describe the perfect waterfall.

While walking an ocean beach, _____ washes up at your feet.

Craft Sparks

You collect a bag of stones for divination.

You plan a new wand or stave.

What is your time of greatest power?

You consider becoming a magickal mentor, or teacher.

You draw a tarot card.

A magickal family member gifts you with a precious talisman.

You explore a sacred text.

You steep an infusion. How does it look? Smell? Taste?

You receive mysteries at an initiation.

You open a Book of Shadows. Describe one of the pages.

You cast runes. What do they tell you?
You imagine designing the perfect *sanctum sanctorum*.

Fantasy Sparks

You sit in an open rowboat, gliding toward a magickal island.
You are a magickal creature. Describe yourself.
You stand within the Great Hall of a magickal school.
A deity appears before you. What do you say?
You find evidence that a faery has visited your home.
Consider the Children of the Night.
You are invisible.
You can fly.
Create a "coin of the realm."
You take part in a magickal banquet.
If you had one fantastic power, what would it be?

Personal Sparks

Recall the day you met your greatest love.
You engage in a self-healing ritual.
Describe one thing you will do in the next ten years.
If you could change one thing in the world, what would it be?
Recall the first time you knew you'd worked magick.
Recall a special pet, or familiar.
"I never knew what _____ meant, until I _____."
Pay homage to a favorite writer, magickal or mundane.
Open your magickal kit: what's inside?
Reflect on a favorite written work.
Write about a hero of yours.

Miscellaneous

As part of a magickal initiation, you receive a tattoo.
You consider your totem or spirit animals.

Describe a piece of magickal jewelry or a talisman.

What does magick mean to you?

Consider your zodiacal sun sign.

You're on a quest; what do you seek?

Describe your *sanctum sanctorum*.

You bite into a magick apple.

You spend a night sleeping under the stars.

You wave a magick wand: what happens?

You're at a public ritual.

You sit with friends around a blazing campfire.

You watch a sunset (or sunrise).

You stand before the writer's guild, asking to be tested.

fifteen

WRITING SPELLWORK AND RITUAL

If magick is a way of changing reality by working with as many of the corresponding realities as possible, then a spell, prayer, or ritual is a specific set of actions designed to control those realities and alter probability. Reality and magick are, after all, old friends. Many magickal elders and a good number of physicists today believe that the nebulous field of quantum mechanics may finally locate the intersection between magick and science. Until that day comes, let's agree that magick is the means of affecting probability in order to achieve a desired outcome. This is the aim of all magickal ritual and spellwork.

WRITING SPELLS

Crafting a spell involves these steps:

1. Determine your goals and intention.

2. Select the spell's components.

3. Outline the spell and its details.

4. Carry it out.

5. Record and evaluate the results.

Let's imagine that your goal is to write a spell of empowerment and blessing for a special writing pen. You decide to use lunar symbolism for its associations with emotions and right-brain work. A few relevant correspondences include Monday, the full moon, the colors of silver and white, moonstone, quartz, and sandalwood incense (Chapter 16 will go further into correspondences).

Using the above steps, your outline might look like this:

1. Conduct the spell under a waxing or full moon, and on a Monday, if possible.

2. Assemble the following materials: the pen, a 12-inch square of silver or white fabric, matches, sandalwood incense, a white candle, a small decorative cup or cauldron of water, a 9-inch piece of purple ribbon or cording.

3. Wash hands and face before beginning. Meditate briefly on the spell's intention.

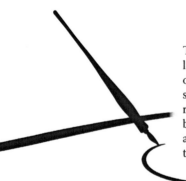

𝒲RITER'S GRIMOIRE

The term "left brain" refers to the logical, intellect-driven aspects of thought, controlled by the left side of the brain. "Right brain" refers to functions ruled by the brain's right side: emotion, creativity, the subconscious, and all things artistic.

4. Spread the fabric square and set the pen on its center. Light the incense and the candle and say, **"May the powers of earth fill this pen."**

5. Pass the pen through the incense cloud and say, **"May the powers of air fill this pen."**

6. Pass the pen over the candle flame and say, **"May the powers of fire fill this pen."**

7. Dip your fingers into the water and brush the pen and say, **"May the powers of water fill this pen."**

8. Finally, hold the pen to your heart and say, **"May the power of my spirit fill this pen."**

9. Repeat the following:

    By all the pow'rs of earth and moon,
    Through every hour, from noon 'til noon,
    Gift this pen with words of might,
    A wealth of ideas soon to write.

10. Wrap the pen in the cloth and tie closed with the purple cord. Store like this in your *sanctum* when not using.

Write the spell into your magickal journal or Book of Shadows for future use. Don't skip the evaluation phase—make sure to consider how well the spell works, how easy it was to enact, etc. Write your comments and observations in your Book of Shadows.

WRITING A POEM

Did you notice the little poem in the above spell? Many spells, chants, and rituals use poetry. A poem is a piece of writing that is often rhythmical, usually metaphorical, and includes formal poetic elements, like meter, rhyme, and stanzaic structure. Poems suggest both speech and music, and most arouse the reader's emotions through the feelings created by the words, or the beauty of the words themselves.

Earlier in the book, we agreed that everyone *can* be taught to write. Not all of us will be an Ernest Hemingway or a Toni Morrison, but we all can learn to put our thoughts down on paper. It's the same for poetry: the muse may gift only a handful of Walt Whitmans or Sylvia Plaths, but each of us has the ability to work with words and ideas, and to forge the beginnings of simple poetry.

So, how to start writing poetry? I must tell you, dear reader, that I am not a poet, and that providing a course in poetry in the space of these pages is beyond the capabilities of this book or its writer. But I would like to provide a quick overview of some of poetry's basic components, as well as a couple of ideas on how to take the plunge into becoming, as a seven-year-old friend once called it, a "poemist."

First, you must write about something that matters to you. It can be happy, odd, confusing, magickal, or sad—but it must matter. Second, you must pick up the pen and start writing. Once your ideas are on paper, you can revise and reshape them—but until you begin, the poem can't happen.

Once the first draft of your poem is on the paper, play with it. Poets love to lace their words with different meanings, and you should embellish your starter poem with image-rich words. Use a thesaurus or rhyming dictionary to find fresh ideas; for example, synonyms for *story* might include *narrative, account, anecdote, yarn, spiel, scenario,* or *libretto.* When choosing words, consider both denotative and connotative word meanings.

The basic unit of the poem is the line; put a group of lines together and you have a stanza. Poems may have one or more stanzas, separated visually by white space. Your poem may range from a few words to several pages in length.

A poem's sense of rhythm is created by several effects, including (a) the way the words seem to flow, stress, and pause; (b) the grammar; (c) the syllables; (d) the length and varied structure of the sentences; (e) the meter; (f) the presence or absence of rhyme; and (g) the use of figurative language.

Meter refers to stresses and pauses that affect the poem's words at regular, fixed intervals. There are four basic kinds of metric feet in poetry (Table 1):

Table 1. Basic Poetic Feet

The iamb	An unstressed syllable followed by a **stressed** syllable	By **all** / the **pow'rs** / of **earth** / and **moon** "By **all**" is an iambic foot.
The anapest	Two unstressed syllables followed by a **stressed** syllable	Now **this** / is the **law** / of the **jun-** / gle (Rudyard Kipling) "Is the **law**" is an anapestic foot.
The trochee	A **stressed** syllable followed by an unstressed syllable	**Dou**-ble / **dou**-ble / **toil** and / **trou**-ble (William Shakespeare) "**Dou**-ble" is a trochaic foot.
The dactyl	A **stressed** syllable followed by two unstressed syllables	**Pus**-sy cat / **pus**-sy cat / **where** have you / **been** (Mother Goose) "**Pus**-sy cat" is a dactylic foot.

*W*RITER'S
GRIMOIRE

A word's denotative meaning is its dictionary definition, while its connotative meaning refers to additional overtones or suggestions the word gains in other contexts. In denotative terms, a skeleton is the body's bony framework. But the word *skeleton* also has connotations of death, thinness, and disease.

Meter is further defined by how many feet occur within a line:

One foot per line = monometer
Two feet per line = dimeter
Three feet per line = trimeter
Four feet per line = tetrameter
Five feet per line = pentameter
Six feet per line = hexameter (and so forth)

In metric terms, poems are described in terms of the type of foot and the number of feet per line. For example, let's look at the beginning of the short poem from the above spell, with the stressed syllables underlined:

By **all** the **pow'rs** of **earth** and **moon,**
Through **every** **hour,** from **noon** 'til **noon,**

The basic foot is an iamb, and there are four iambs in each line. Therefore, the above poem is an example of iambic tetrameter. See if you can give the correct poetic meter, in type of foot and number of feet, for this line (see answer at bottom of page):

Dou-ble / **dou**-ble / **toil** and / **trou**-ble

Some writers prefer to create rhyming poetry, while others prefer freeform (non-rhyming) verse. The choice is yours. While most poetry today is freeform, many magick users prefer rhyming poems for spell, charm, and ritual use, as the rhyme and meter affect the listener and set a mood that supports the formality of the magickal undertaking. Rhyming also makes memorization easier.

As the poem comes along, read your own work out loud. How do the words sound together? How do the word-images and phrases affect you? How does the rhythm feel to your ear? Experiment

A: Did you say trochaic tetrameter? If you did, you're right!

with word substitution, then read the results aloud and listen to how the sound of each line changes.

Get outside feedback by asking a friend or first reader to read and comment on your newborn poem. Tuck the work away for two or more days, then pull it out, and read it again.

For further exploration of poetic forms, please look through the resources section. I particularly recommend Elizabeth Barrette's book, *Composing Magic*, which presents a detailed course in poetry as a form of magickal writing and ritual.

WRITING CHANTS

Chants are a form of sung or spoken, repeated, rhythmic poetry, often set to music. The word *chant* comes from the Latin *encantare*, meaning "to sing," and many religious and magickal traditions include sung or spoken chants in their worship and ritual. Chants may vary in length from short to long, and are often repeated for a set period of time throughout a ritual, dance, or spell.

Why use chant? Through sound and rhythm, chant adds a mystical, otherworldly effect to a ritual. Even more important, chants allow audience participation, which helps build group energy and raise power within the magickal space. For a solitary practitioner,

*W*RITER'S
GRIMOIRE

Euphony is the pleasant sound words make as they work together. In contrast, cacophony is sound created by harsh, discordant words.

chanting can help create a feeling of both power and magickal space, while enhancing and enriching the mood.

Chants take one of three forms:

Unison chant: repeated by all participants, simultaneously.

Call and response chant: the leader reads or sings the main portion of the chant, and the audience replies with a response, chorus, or refrain.

Staged chant: certain "players" sing or speak the chant to create a planned dramatic effect, often as part of a ritual. For heightened effect, the chanters may be hidden "off stage."

In a group, chanting is usually led or directed by a leader. The chant may end with a burst of focused or directed energy, e.g., an emphatic shout with or without a physical gesture, such as a rapid upraising of the hands toward the sky. In magickal workings relating to warding, banishing, releasing, etc., the chant may be repeated more and more softly, until it becomes a soft echo and fades away.

To write a chant, begin by considering your intention, and why you want to create the chant. How and where will you use it? Will you use the chant as a solitary, or will it be part of a group activity? Will it be spoken or sung? Work through those questions, then follow these simple steps:

*M*AGICKAL
MENTION

The magickal word *enchant* shares the same *encantare* root as the word *chant*, but means something more along the lines of "to put the senses under a spell with song."

1. Choose a theme or central idea for your chant. In general, chants work best with a vivid or powerful central idea: a Sabbat, a season, a deity, etc.

2. Jot down ideas and words that you want to include. Let's imagine you wanted to write a chant for sitting a Yule vigil fire and greeting the morning sun. You might want to focus on words like *bonfire, balefire, cold, winter, sun, light,* etc.

3. Start with a simple rhythm—trochaic meter works well for chants; placing the force on initial syllables helps add a sense of drumming power to the words.

4. Start by writing the first line, then expand your chant by one line at a time. Chants work best when they rhyme, as this adds to the vocal power and meter of what is essentially a spoken or sung poem. Speak the words aloud as you go, balancing rhythm and rhyme as needed. An online rhyming dictionary will help you fit sound and meter together.

Here's an example of a simple winter vigil chant, with emphases indicated:

> **On** this **eve**ning
> **Wood** and **cir**cle **ga**ther,
> **Sit** the **bale**fire,
> **Mind** the **win**ter **wea**ther.
> **Hold** the **vi**gil
> **As** the fire **bu**rns—
> **Hark**: the **sun**rise
> **Now** the **light** re**turns**!

WRITING A MAGICKAL MEDITATION

Writing a meditation is like writing a simple story in the second person point of view. The typical meditation begins with a serene setting—a meadow, garden, forest, etc.—and guides the reader through it. The listener's journey becomes a metaphor for the journey taken within his mind, as he travels deeper within himself and enters an altered state.

A key difference between story and meditation is that the meditation doesn't have rising tension or a final crisis. The goal of meditation is to instill a sense of equanimity and peacefulness. Most meditations end up sending the participant on a short journey and then, as the meditation ends, circling them back to where they began.

When crafting meditation, include lots of multisensory imagery: this enriches the setting and can assist the listener in entering a meditative state. Keep your sentences fairly short and all about the same length; this creates rhythm and adds to the "hypnotic" mood within the meditation.

Here's a short example:

> *You stand on a path. Ahead of you, the path leads into an open forest. It is morning; the sun is still low in the sky, and the air is cool and fresh. You can hear birds singing around you, and the air is rich with the scent of flowers. Walking slowly ahead, you enter the forest. It is peaceful here, and quiet. The air feels damp. The forest floor is soft under your feet, a springy carpet of green moss. As you walk farther into the forest, you're aware of giant trees rising to either side. You notice a soft light in the distance. As you walk toward it, the path opens into a clearing. In the center of the clearing is a crystalline blue pool of water. You kneel and then sit down on the ground next to the pool. As you gaze into the pool, a feeling of peace steals over you . . . . (etc.)*

WRITING PRAYERS AND BLESSINGS

Prayers and blessings are pieces of writing—usually fairly short—in which the user attempts to access or channel divine energy. Our urge to pray may spring from a perceived need or may simply reflect our desire to connect with the divine around us. The motivation to bestow blessings may arise from request, inspiration, or from one's position of authority within a spiritual group.

In **prayers**, a deity, patron, or divine energy is welcomed, thanked, acknowledged, or invited to give its blessings or protection. The energy begins with the person speaking the prayer and is sent outward, into the universe and into the realm of the divine.

When writing a prayer, begin by considering your intention or request. Consider, too, whom you will pray to—for the best result, do your research and identify the most appropriate deity or patron, as well as the one that is meaningful to you.

Open the prayer with an address: "Dear _____," "Most honorable _____," etc. Keep the body of the prayer relevant and reasonably brief. Humans don't like it when appeals are gushily overstated, and the gods and goddesses probably don't either. Finish with a simple closing and a thank you, or with a signal word or phrase that shows you're finished, e.g., "Blessed Be.".

*M*AGICKAL MENTION

Working with energy can be difficult or even hazardous for the untrained. If energy work is new to you, please consult a magickal source or teacher for guidance in learning basic concepts of grounding, centering, meditating, shielding, auric work, chakra balancing, and more.

Blessings are used to give approval, consecration, initiation, thanks, or beneficence. The energy is, in effect, pulled from the universe and bestowed upon a recipient.

Crafting and offering blessings is a little more challenging. When you give a blessing, you tap directly into and channel a well of divine energy. If you have received an initiation or attunement in a magickal tradition, you may have also received access to a reservoir of energy. If not, don't worry—all of us have the ability to manipulate energy directly from the universe.

Writing a blessing is similar to crafting a prayer. The simplest blessings may consist of a few words spoken over food, or upon awakening in the morning, such as:

> *Another day, begun for me,*
> *Greet the morning—*
> *Blessed be!*

Even the words "Blessed be," or "Bright blessings," spoken by many of us every day—and even used to conclude phone calls and e-mails—create an informal blessing.

For a longer, more serious blessing, begin with an address or welcome. Identify yourself, state your intentions, give the blessing, and acknowledge the support or gifts of any related deities or patrons. Finish with a simple phrase or signal words that indicate your conclusion: "So mote it be" and "Many blessings" are examples.

> *Blessed Gaia,*
> *you give me food*
> *that I may never hunger.*
> *You give me water*
> *that I may not thirst.*
> *May I be worthy,*
> *and always keep the balance.*
> *Many blessings!*

Always consider the setting in which you'll deliver the prayer or blessing. As with any ritualized activity, think about timing, correspondences, and your own readiness. Pray and offer blessings when you are rested and unstressed, and with the proper humility and genuineness of spirit. It also goes without saying that from an ethical standpoint, you must believe in the motivations driving the action. Ground and center before and after to replenish your own energy supply. If appealing to certain deities, the donning of appropriate colors or jewelry, the lighting of incense, the use of specific hand gestures, or other outward signs may be appropriate. Blessings may likewise be coupled with a physical gesture or action, such as a laying on of hands, the giving of a piece of ritual garb, or the bestowal of a title.

WRITING A RITUAL

A ritual is a ceremony or series of actions performed in a specific order and for a specific purpose. Rituals may be simple or complex and may involve any number of people or even a solitary participant. Some rituals are performed to honor unique or special occasions, such as a college graduation, a magickal initiation, or a birthday. Some rituals are part of our daily routine, as in the steps taken in brewing a cup of tea as part of a meditation. Neither the tea preparation nor the meditation alone compose a ritual; but when combined with intention and purpose, a ritual takes shape.

The formality and specific nature of your ritual will depend on your aims and on your own magickal traditions, but all rituals require you to consider these points:

- Begin with an **overall theme**—a big idea defining the ritual's focus. Who or what will it celebrate or honor? What is the ritual's purpose or intention?

- Once your theme is set, plan the **components or steps** in the ritual, e.g., site preparation, the altar space, calling quarters, inviting deities, the creation of sacred space, the raising of power, music, symbolism, etc.

- With a plan in place, consider the **specific details**. Where will you hold the ritual? What about correspondences, deities, season, moon phase, etc.? Who will take part? How long will the ritual last? Is special garb required? Include the spoken parts: openings, invocations, blessings, quarter calls, chants, and more.

- Last but not least—the **fine-tuning**. Who will bring the cakes and ale? Will you have time to practice the chant before the event? Is there a rain plan?

In writing the ritual, create a detailed plan that includes every possible aspect. Add a list at the end for unanswered questions, and make margin notes about how you will fit specific people into the plan. When finished, proofread carefully.

Not all rituals need to be written down. But crafting a ritual in written form has benefits: it gives participants an easy way to understand and study their roles, allows the ritual to be saved for future reuse, and allows easy evaluation of the ritual after it's completed.

TO MEMORIZE OR NOT TO MEMORIZE

Is it necessary to memorize a spell or ritual in order for it to work? No, it's not. But memorizing does have some advantages. First, if you lose the paper with the spell written on it, you'll still be able to perform. Second, by memorizing your part in a spell or ritual, the words enter your memory and unconscious, internalizing the spell in your mind and potentially making it more powerful. Third, by committing the spell to memory, you can recite it aloud during the ritual or working, leaving your hands free to work with tools or carry out other aspects of the magickal act. And most important, by not having to read from a piece of paper, you will be less distracted and more able to enter into the magick of the experience.

INSPIRATION

Use the following suggestions to inspire your inner magickal writer when crafting spellwork and rituals:

- Activate the power of scent. Burn incense, diffuse oil, light scented candles, bring in a vase of sweet peas or lilacs, etc.

- Before writing, spend a few minutes reading from a book of magickal prayer or poetry for inspiration (see Resources).

- Make a ritual of brewing a cup of herbal tea to sip as you write. Envision the rising steam filling you with inspiration.

- Play music: chant, Native American flute music, and Celtic music are evocative for many magick uses. Experiment with different music to see how it affects your mood and writing.

- Surround yourself with a specific element or color.

- Wear magickal jewelry or regalia.

- When you're outdoors, search for "places of power." Use these as writing locations.

- Write after taking a hot, oil-scented bath.

- Write at certain times of the day (daybreak or sunset, perhaps), or on certain days of the week.

- Write at unusual times, or in unusual places.

- Write by moonlight, candlelight, or firelight.

_Scribbulus_ _____

1. What spiritual tradition do you follow? Does it have ancient or hereditary roots? Write a ritual, spell, or other piece of written magick in keeping with your own traditions.

2. Create a name or title for one of your personal magickal or writing texts or journals. Develop a spell or ritual and officially bestow the name or title.

3. Search through your magickal or writer's journal for an interesting moment or bit of insight. Write a poem about that moment or insight.

4. Write a simple blessing to use before meals.

sixteen

MAGICKAL CORRESPONDENCES FOR WRITERS

In this chapter, we'll explore the intersections of writing and magick, looking at correspondences, patrons, and other magick-relevant considerations.

USING THE ELEMENTS

The Sicilian philosopher Empedocles (fifth century BCE) is credited with developing the concept of four elements as the basis of all life and being in the universe. These ideas found a prominent place in Aristotle's teachings (384–322 BCE), informed the Pythagorean Mysteries of ancient Greece, and eventually became foundational in all Western systems from the Middle East, Egypt, Greece, and Rome, on into Hermetics, alchemy, and modern witchcraft and wizardry. The following are writer-based suggestions; you can adjust these to mesh with your own traditions.

Earth (north/winter): Physical existence and constancy; prosperity; abundance; the beasts. To invoke this element, use stones, crystals, fossils, bones, seeds, or potted plants. Create a stone writer's talisman to empower your work. The earth-writer's tool is a pen or pencil of wood or stone.

Air (east/spring): Intellect and communication; mystery; the birds. To invoke this element, use feathers, pumice stones, silk, catkins, airborne seeds, bits of spider webs, wind chimes, and small bells. Grow a potted peace lily on your desk (these plants cleanse the air in a four-foot space around the plant). Open the window and allow the winds of inspiration to blow through. Select and consecrate a special writing quill to your purposes. The air-writer's tool is a fine quill, consecrated to your intentions.

Fire (south/summer): Passion and creativity; the stars. To invoke this element, use sun-dried herbs, gourds, ashes, charcoal, volcanic rock, thundereggs, and sun-charged

*M*AGICKAL MENTION

A burning candle is the most perfect of all magickal tools, containing all four elements simultaneously. The solid waxen candle itself is earth; the melted wax represents water; the gaseous smoke becomes air; and the glowing flame is fire. Use a candle anointed or scented with an essential oil bound to your intention, and you have an ideal tool for magickal writing. (Just keep your papers away from the candle flame!)

waters. Burn candles or incense. The fire-writer's tool is a set of art supplies in brilliant colors.

Water (west/autumn): Compassion, emotion, and transformation; the fish. To invoke this element, use vials of charged waters, cacti and succulent plants, petrified rock, polished agates and river stones, and seashells. If you have the space, add a small fountain to one corner of your writing space. The water-writer's tool is a set of brilliant inks, held in a crystalline bottle or inkwell to let the inks' colors shine through.

CORRESPONDENCES AND MAGICKAL WRITING

As with any form of magickal practices, meshing your intentions with the relevant correspondences is fun and boosts your written and magickal results. Do you want to give voice to your passions on a subject? Sit out at noon on a sunny Wednesday; face and invoke the watchtowers of the south while sipping orange juice and writing with red ink. Interested in sharpening your memory? Try writing at dusk while brewing peppermint tea, wearing moonstones, and working with blue ink or paper.

Color Magick

Colors can be used to inspire and enhance writing—think in terms of ink, colored pens, paper, notebooks, and magickal influence:

Black: banishing, warding, reversals, hexing, solace, dark moon spells, power

Blue: powerful protection, wards against the evil eye, healing

Brown: grounding, centering, stability, endurance, fairness, judgment

Gold: wealth, prosperity, achievement, royalty, god work, sun spells

Green: growth, creativity, nature, fertility, balance, abundance, prosperity, calm

Indigo: intellect, insight, clairvoyance, prescience

Orange: health, vigor, energy, creativity, enthusiasm

Pink: love, friendship, romance, community, children

Purple: sex, passion, power, domination, wisdom, higher consciousness

Red: sex, love, passion, fertility, protection against danger, power, strength, war

Silver: goddess work, insight, magick in general, full moon spells

White: purity, innocence, initiation, ghosts and spirits, ancestors, general moon spells

Yellow: power, protection, divination, intellect, prosperity

Herbal Magick

There are many ways to use herbal magick in your writing. Leave pinches of protective herbs in the drawers or boxes where you store your writing tools, or use herbs to guard your books. When you begin a writing session, burn a scented candle, diffuse a bit of oil, or set out a dish of potpourri. Sip an herbal infusion to fill yourself with the desired intention. Slip a drop or two of essential oil into your favorite ink mixture or use infused waters to craft your own inks. Anoint your writing tools with a fingertip touched to oil or infusion.

Here are some useful herbal correspondences for the magickal writer:

Abundance: allspice

Alertness: mint

Astral protection: mugwort

Communication: fennel

Confidence: ginger

Courage: borage

Divination: dandelion, St. John's wort

Dream work: lavender, marigold, mugwort

Grounding: rosemary, thyme

Insight: chamomile, rosemary

Inspiration: clove, ginger, lemon balm

Magick: rosemary, sage

Medicinal use (via infusion): catnip (relieves headaches), chamomile (relieves stress and tension), evening primrose (relieves stress and tension), lavender (relaxes, relieves tension), St. John's wort (relieves headache and tension)

Mental powers: caraway, honeysuckle, horehound, lilac, mace, mint, rosemary, summer savory, walnut

Prophecy: calendula, marigold

Prosperity: allspice

Protection: birch, evening primrose, horehound, marigold, mugwort, rosemary, sage, wormwood

Psychic powers: bay, borage, calendula, cinnamon, mace, marigold, mugwort, rosemary, rowan, thyme, wormwood, yarrow

Purification: hyssop, dandelion, lavender, lemon, rosemary, sage, thyme

Self-expression: fennel

Shielding: evening primrose, rosemary

Spirit (and muse) calling: dandelion

Success: clove, ginger

Wishes: dandelion, sage, walnut

Stone and Metal Magick

For a writer, stones or bits of metal can become powerful talismans within the writing space. A specially picked, cleansed, and charged stone makes a powerful (and useful!) magickal paperweight: see below for a suggestion on making your own. A polished stone can be used as an artist's tool to rub or smudge work in charcoal, pastel, colored pencil, or crayon. Stones may also be used in charms and spells, on your altar, or simply to decorate your writing space. Many of us also have favorite magickal jewelry that includes special stones or crystals.

Select stones and crystals for the energies and correspondences they bring to your writing practices. Here are some simple stone correspondences that may find use in your writing space:

Creativity: actinolite, aventurine, calcite, carnelian, citrine, pyrite, sapphire, topaz, tourmaline

Diminishing negativity: amethyst, black jade, jasper, malachite, obsidian, peridot, smoky quartz, tourmaline

Dissipating tension: bronze, calcite, carnelian, fluorite, lepidolite, peridot

Grounding: calcite, hematite, iron, jasper, moonstone, obsidian, silver, smoky quartz, sodalite, tiger's eye, tourmaline

Imagination: aventurine, Herkimer diamonds

Logic: fluorite, pyrite, sodalite

Memory: carnelian, emerald, gold calcite, pyrite, quartz (clear), yellow sapphire

Mental powers: fluorite, hematite, turquoise

Protection: citrine, copper, coral, diamond, emerald, flint, garnet, jade, jet, lapis, marble, moss agate, quartz (clear), ruby

Psychic awareness: amethyst, citrine, fluorite, quartz (clear), sapphire, silver, sugilite, tiger's eye, topaz

Stress reduction: amethyst, lace agate, peridot, sodalite

TIMING

In writing, as in magick, timing is everything. The time of year, the time of day, the month, the season, the Wheel of the Year, the cycling of the plant and animal life, and even the positions of heavenly bodies have powerful magickal influences. As magickal practitioners, we try to work within or at least alongside these forces. For instance, we know that initiations are best done at a spring sunrise, when natural energies support birth and new beginnings. We understand that a dark moon in the depths of winter is a powerful time of silence, a time to plant metaphorical seeds and magick that

*M*AGICKAL
MENTION
Visit bead stores or online rock and bead shops to purchase strings containing hundreds of polished stone and crystal chips for only a few dollars. These tiny chips work well as beads for magickal garb or jewelry. They're also ideal in spellwork, charms, or charged waters, and can be stored in decorative glass vials.

will take root and blossom in months to come. Likewise, efforts made to mesh your writerly workings with the natural forces surrounding you will empower your prose, enchant your charms, and elevate your rituals.

Time of Day

Depending on your own internal clock and the content of your writing project, the time of day you choose for writing can play a role in the magick:

> *Dawn*: A time to contemplate new beginnings, fresh starts, and rebirths, and a powerful time to begin new writing projects. In many traditions, "the last hour before dawn" is the time of faeries.

> *Noon*: A time of balance; also a time when the sun is directly overhead, with its power at a peak. This is the best time to bring your work to fruition.

> *Dusk*: A time of great power, as the sun's energies ebb and give way to those of the moon. This is an excellent time to write spellwork, ritual, and other kinds of magick.

> *Midnight*: Like noon, this is another time of balance, with the sun at its greatest ebb and the heavenly bodies at their maximum power. Midnight is often called "the witching hour." Interesting things appear on the pages of a writer who plies her craft into the dark hours of night.

Day of the Week

The best writers try to write at least as little bit every day, and you might give some thought as to how the correspondences of each day impact an important magickal writing task:

Monday: Moon's Day. A good time for writing about feminine mysteries, birth, initiations, emotion, and compassion.

Tuesday: Tyr's Day, under the rule of Mars. Prime time for writing stories or charms involving strength, courage, heroism, and power.

Wednesday: Woden's (Odin's) Day. Ruled by Mercury, and an ideal time for writing that invokes wisdom, creativity, and divination.

Thursday: Thor's Day. Ruled by Jupiter, this is the best day for magickal work involving luck, success, and prosperity. It's also the best day to submit pieces for potential publication.

Friday: Freya's Day, ruled by Venus. If you want to write about love, romance, friendship, and beauty, today's your day.

Saturday: The god Saturn's Day, also ruled by the planet Saturn. Saturday is ideal for spellwork affecting protection, structure, resolution, partings, and endings.

Sunday: Sun's Day. An optimal day for writing about all things masculine and those involving peace, harmony, success, and divine power.

*M*AGICKAL
MENTION

Create charged waters by allowing a vial or chalice of water to sit outside when the requisite heavenly body is overhead. Use the charged waters in spells, charms, and for ritual infusions and anointing.

WORKING WITH CHARMS AND TALISMANS

Many of the above correspondences can be used to make charms or talismans, specialized types of spellcraft in and of themselves. A **charm** is a like a miniature spell that combines intention and components to send magick out into the world, creating a specific effect. Some magick users define a charm as a spell in which the words are spoken out loud. A charm's energy reaches outward, extending away from the charm caster. Most charms work for a set time period and then cease.

A **talisman** is an object that either is embodied with naturally occurring magick or is intentionally charged with magick via a spell or charm. Talismans are a sort of storage battery for energy, drawing energy inward toward the talisman's wearer or bearer. Talismans are often linked to a specific deity, or to a branch of elemental energy. They are typically worn, carried, or displayed by the person seeking the magickal effect. Most talismans work indefinitely.

Writer's Charm

1. Begin with a 6-inch square of white fabric (the four sides represent the four elements).

2. On that fabric, place one or two pieces of citrine or hematite, a sprig of rosemary, and some fresh shavings from a pencil you write with.

3. Add a small piece of paper on which you've inscribed several stars. Recite the following:

   Gathered here, within this square,
   Signs of creative power.
   Embolden thus my magick craft,
   That I may write the hours.

4. Tie the fabric square shut and place it on your desk, or in the location that you do most of your writing. When you sit down to write, imagine that energy is pouring from the charm, ready to inspire your writing.

5. Each time you sit down to write, hold the charm in your hand and repeat the above rhyme. This will recharge the charm, allowing it to work indefinitely.

Writer's Talisman: A Ritual

Select a stone of your choice—it can be one with a writing correspondence, or simply one that you find pleasing. Cleanse the stone (see below), then charge by placing it on your altar or under sun- or moonlight for another twenty-four hours.

When you're ready to empower the talisman, dissolve some sea salt in a small bowl of water, and light a candle. Dip your fingertips into the salt water and anoint the stone as you repeat the following:

I bless this stone with water.
May the waters of inspiration flow through me!

*M*AGICKAL
MENTION

Use the elements to cleanse your magickal tools and materials:

- Earth: Bury the item in salt, sand, or soil.

- Air: Smudge the item with burning herbs or incense.

- Fire: Pass the item above a candle flame, or place it in direct sunlight.

- Water: Immerse the item in spring, well, or charged waters.

I bless this stone with the salt of the earth.
May earth's constancy embolden me!

Now pass the stone above the candle flame as you repeat the following:

I bless this stone with air.
May air's transcendence blow through me!

I bless this stone with fire.
May the passions of fire inspire me!

Earth, air, fire, and water, now held within this stone.
May they gift me with energy and joy as I ply my craft.

Set the stone on your desk. Whenever you begin a writing session, hold the stone into your hand or over your crown chakra and imagine the stored energies flowing through you. Using it as a paperweight will instill the same charge in your books and papers. You might also use your stone talisman when invoking your own muse.

DEITIES AND PATRONS FOR WRITERS

Are you interested in appealing to a protective or supportive patron? Here are a few, listed in alphabetical order. Note that this includes a handful of patron saints, many of whom are referenced by both magickal and non-magickal writers:

Athena (Athene, Greek) is an ancient goddess associated with wisdom, learning, and writing. Her totem is the owl; if you wish for Athena to inspire your craft, you might search for a small owl to add to your writing space.

Bran the Blessed (Welsh, pan-Celtic) is one of the Celtic gods of writing.

Brigit (Irish) is a Celtic goddess of poetry. Her Catholic doppelganger, St. Brigid, is likewise a patron saint of poets. In either guise, Brigit's affiliation with hearth and forge stokes a writer's creative fires.

In the Catholic church, *Francis de Sales, John the Apostle*, and *Paul the Apostle* are patron saints of writers and poets, while *Cecilia, Columba*, and *David* are patron saints of poets.

Odin (Norse) could be called a god of writing, for it was through Odin that we received the runes and the runic alphabet.

Oghma (Scottish, Irish) is called the Celtic god of communication, writing, and poetry. He is said to have invented the Ogham tree alphabet and then to have given it to the Druids.

Two Egyptian goddesses were associated with writing. *Sefkhet-Abwy* was the goddess of writing and of the temple libraries, and *Seshat* was the goddess of writing, communication, and measurements.

Thoth (Egyptian) is a patron god of magick, writing, and the moon.

As a writer, your favorite authors, writers, and teachers are also powerful patrons, and even muse-symbols. Do you want to create characters like Stephen King, craft an epic à la Tolkien, tell a personal story like Phyllis Curott, or speak of magick like Starhawk? Invoke their names in your magickal workings, thanking them for their skills and their example. (Look back at Chapter 5 for details on invoking the muse.)

Scribbulus

1. Select several favorite correspondences. Devote a writing journal page to each one, and begin collecting information for later use.

2. Develop a correspondence set that matches your elemental alignment as determined by your birth/sun sign. Earth: Capricorn, Taurus, and Virgo. Air: Aquarius, Gemini, and Libra. Fire: Aries, Leo, and Sagittarius. Water: Pisces, Cancer, and Scorpio.

3. Create a "kit" of basic materials for spellcraft and magick. For example, a basic kit might include salt, charged water, rosemary, candles in several colors, a 9-foot cord (for outlining a magick circle), a compass, some chalk, and two or three stones of your choice. Add a pocket-sized spiral notebook, a pen, and some matches. Keep the kit in a plastic baggie, tucked into your pocket or purse.

seventeen

MAGICK BY THE BOOK

In the simplest terms, a book is a collection of written, illustrated, or blank sheets, bound together within a cover. But as we know, a book is much, much more. Books hold stories, images, wisdom, music, poetry, magick . . . . Between a book's covers is a world waiting to be explored. Open a book and it's as if you've used one of Madeleine L'Engle's tesseracts to teleport away to a different time and place. If it's true that a person's beliefs and ideas determine how they live, the real magick of books may be in their timelessness and their ability to seamlessly connect the past and present, the magickal and mundane.

BOOKCRAFTING: EARLY HISTORY

The earliest form of book was the scroll, dating back to several centuries BCE, but the first real books were the codexes, arising near the beginning of the common era (see Chapter 10 for details). Much of what we think of today as the modern book took shape during the Roman Empire. After Rome fell, books were crafted or hand-copied in medieval monasteries, sometimes in special rooms called scriptoriums. Artificial light and fire were forbidden in the scribing space for fear of damaging the manuscripts.

Within scriptoriums, the copy work was done by monk-scribes working in one of several roles. Copyists handled the basic transcription, while calligraphers inscribed the finest or most expensive books. The finished work was collated and edited by correctors, who compared the end result with the original source text. Rubricators painted in the large red letters that headed each section, and illuminators added borders, illustrations, and other textual decorations.

From that point, bookbinders collated and bound the pages and adorned the covers. Bookbinding was and is an arcane craft; even today, becoming a bookbinder means taking on a long apprenticeship and learning to work with specialized tools and practices that have changed little since the Middle Ages.

The process of making books was controlled in medieval times by stationer's craft guilds, via the traditional apprentice-journeyman-master process. With the advent of the printing press, the

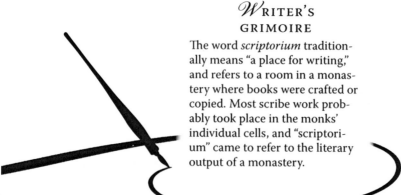

*W*RITER'S GRIMOIRE

The word *scriptorium* traditionally means "a place for writing," and refers to a room in a monastery where books were crafted or copied. Most scribe work probably took place in the monks' individual cells, and "scriptorium" came to refer to the literary output of a monastery.

guilds lost their hold on the publishing industry. Today, we stand on the brink of even greater changes in publishing, as the computer age and desktop publication have made authoring and publishing books available to anyone with the patience and inclination to set words to paper.

BOOKS AND MAGICK

Books are often considered powerful because of their history (being handed down through a family or a coven), their contents, or their holy nature. The words "it is written" are a traditional proclamation, and may have led directly to the magickal "so mote it be." Naming something is a potent way of empowering it, and many books have gained notoriety and strength over millennia, largely because of their names. For instance, simply calling a magickal text a Book of Shadows conjures up layers of meanings and implies that the text possesses innate power as well as magickal connections.

Magick practitioners tend to embrace the mystical powers of the written word, and our magickal history is filled with an array of fascinating texts, as well as a trove of myth and mystery. Bits of magickal writings attributed to Solomon are said to still exist today, kept under secret guard. Caches of papyri inscribed with magickal spells have been uncovered in Alexandria. Certain arcane traditions, including Druidry and alchemy, still pass knowledge and mysteries through allegorical story. Recently, Druid priestess Ellen Evert Hopman created a novel (*Priestess of the Forest*) that serves as both a historical story and an introduction to Druidic teachings.

Those of us who work magick often refer to books as part of our practices, and we sometimes use texts directly in spellwork. Words of a spell or incantation may be written into a magickal journal or Book of Shadows, and reading them aloud then releases their magick into the world. If a book is read aloud during ritual, particularly over elemental ingredients, those ingredients are felt to have been imbued with the power of the words, and the items may then be burned, ingested, smoked, or made into a charm or talisman. A book that is repeatedly used in magickal craft takes on traces of the magick itself and develops its own powers. In a book that is inherently powerful, simply reading from the book becomes an act of magick. Throughout history, the power of some books has been considered so frightening to those in power that the texts have become a focus or fulcrum of political and religious action. In 1557, the medieval Roman Catholic Church created and enforced the *Index Librorum Prohibitum*, a list of prohibited books. Anyone who dared read a book from the list faced excommunication.

In the sixteenth century, the *Malleus Maleficarum* (Latin for "Hammer of the Witches") provided a medieval treatise on witchcraft, as well as the criteria for identifying and killing suspected Witches. And we've all heard the story of the Nazi book-burnings. Even today, lists of banned books persist in the United States, and people fight to have certain books removed from schools. Each of these acts exists because of fear over a book's power to influence readers' thoughts and ideas.

WRITING, BOOKS, AND DIVINATION

Oscar Wilde once wrote, "There is no such thing as an omen. Destiny does not send us heralds. She is too wise or too cruel for that."

𝒲RITER'S GRIMOIRE
The *Index Librorum Prohibitum* was repealed by the Catholic Church on June 14, 1966.

Yet, we writers have found interesting ways to link our craft and its tools with the grand unseen.

Bibliomancy is foretelling the future by interpreting a randomly chosen passage from a book, usually a holy book. The term dates back to medieval times, when the practice involved the literal "weighing" of a person's guilt. A person suspected of a crime was placed on giant scales and weighed against the local church's enormous Bible. If he outweighed the good book, he was guilty as charged; if he weighed less, he was free to go.* Today's bibliomancer picks up a book, meditates briefly, then opens the book to a random page, which—if all goes well—offers a message, or perhaps the answer to a question.

In the "Book Test," another kind of bibliomancy, a medium uses a book to communicate with a dead spirit. The spirit gives the medium the name of a book and a specific page number; when consulted, the page contains a message for the dearly departed's family.

Aleuromancy is "written divination by baked goods." (My kind of divination!) This involves either (a) writing a magickal message on an item before it is baked, e.g., a cookie, a pie, a loaf of bread, etc.; (b) embedding a written message into an item that has already been baked, e.g., a fortune cookie or a message hidden in a donut; or (c) embedding a meaningful object in a baked item, e.g., placing a blanched almond into cake batter, with the intention that whoever finds the almond in their cake will reap some sort of luck or reward.

Rhabdomancy is divination that uses a stick. The stick may be used in one of several ways: (a) as a divining rod; (b) in "spin the bottle" fashion, i.e., the stick is spun and a message divined according to where it points when it stops; or (c) the stick is set on end and a message divined according to where it falls and/or points. Writers can work rhabdomancy using a favorite pencil or pen as the stick. I

---

*McKim, Donald K. *Westminster Dictionary of Theological Terms.* Louisville, KY: Westminster John Knox Press, 1996, p. 30.

have a magickal writer-friend who has made a pencil into a pendulum and claims that it works with great authority.

Graphology is the practice of handwriting analysis, in which a person's life and nature are divined by reading and interpreting his handwriting. The theory here is that handwriting works to transmit the unconscious mind into form, giving insights into a person's essential nature. Of course, magick is at work, too . . .

Ink also finds its way into divination. When ink is spilled into a person's palm, the results can be used as a kind of divinatory scrying, with the patterns and lines read as one would read tea leaves. Black ink can also be added to a bowl of water to create a scrying bowl *par excellence.*

Automatic and Trance Writing

Automatic writing is writing directed by a spirit or the subconscious mind. It is sometimes called "trance" writing because the writer may appear to be in a trance. Deep memories and mystical thoughts may be retrieved in this way. Some practitioners believe that the process allows them to touch past lives or energies left by other beings.

Proponents believe that the detached trance state allows a writer to access her subconscious, allowing her to write from her true self, without conscious inhibition. (As we discussed in Chapter 3, freewriting is another way of accessing subconscious thoughts and ideas.) Those who favor trance writing call it a "soul ritual," saying it not only allows unfettered access into one's innermost thoughts, but also access to a bottomless well of energy. (They also claim that automatic writing is great for writer's block.) Some magickal writers practice trance writing as an intentional aspect of their divination practice.

To try trance writing, sit in a quiet, secluded space. Set the mood in whatever way seems best—music, candles, incense, etc. Meditate on your intentions, then quiet your mind and listen, in the stillness, for the quiet voice of your soul. Begin writing when it feels right to do so, and see what emerges. Be aware of the connection between your mind and hand.

The Ouija board—also called a talking board or spirit board—is a variation on automatic writing. Believers say that the user receives and "writes" messages by moving a planchette across a set of letters printed on the board surface. The movements of the planchette are described as automatic and are controlled by the user's subconscious.

Writers and Superstition

Speaking of the mind, would it surprise you to find out that writers tend to be a superstitious bunch? Like the professional athlete who insists on wearing his lucky orange socks for every important game, many writers have a lucky pen, or brew a cup of the same tea blend, served in the same cup, before beginning a writing session. Despite living in the computer age, many writers who have been at it for a while insist on writing by hand or on an old treasured typewriter. A good many writers won't talk about or share a work-in-progress, allowing others to read it only when a final draft has been accomplished. One of my writer-friends stores finished manuscripts in the refrigerator until they can be mailed out; his theory is that the fridge works like a safe, and if the house should happen to burn down overnight, the manuscript would be safe!

Here are some even stranger writing habits:

- Poet Johann Schiller kept rotten apples in his desk drawer, claiming their scent (or more likely the ethylene gas they gave off while ripening/rotting) helped sharpen his creativity.

- Rudyard Kipling was fanatical about only writing with the purest black ink.

- Dame Edith Sitwell used to precede her day's writing with time spent reclining in an open coffin.

- D. H. Lawrence found authorly inspiration while climbing trees.

- W. H. Auden would drink two dozen cups of tea in a sitting, while Honoré de Balzac drank four dozen cups of coffee. (Poor Balzac eventually died of caffeine poisoning.)

- Benjamin Franklin did some of his best work in the nude or in the bathtub.

- Mark Twain liked to write while lying down, while Virginia Woolf often wrote standing up.

- Marcel Proust built a cork-lined room so that he could write in a soundless setting.

- Robert Frost wrote only at night.

What weird and wonderful writing habits or superstitions will you come up with?

CRAFTING YOUR OWN BOOKS

Are you interesting in making your own books? This can be as simple as cutting out a sheaf of papers and stapling (or sewing) them together, or as complex as studying the fine art of bookbinding. You'll find instructions for either on the Internet, as well as in fascinating "How-To" texts (see Resources). Whatever the size of your handcrafted tome, give it an impressive name. Begin with *Liber ex*, which translates to "Book of." Add a descriptive word in the language of your choice. For example, *Liber ex Somnium*, a "Book of Dreams."

Protecting Your Texts and Writing

The first and simplest means of protecting your *sub rosa* work? Keep your Books of Shadows, Grimoires, and writing journals tucked safely away from the viewing public. Making these tools less accessible is the easiest way to ensure they aren't opened casually.

Another easy fix, mentioned earlier, is to tie your book closed with a ribbon or cord. The tying, untying, and knot work can be made part of a protection ritual, and working with specific colors will add a dimension of correspondences.

You may also want to think about keeping your work safe from insect infestation. Several herbs are believed to repel paper-eating insect pests: these include costmary (balsam), mugwort, wormwood, St. John's Wort, and incense cedar. To use, place completely dried whole leaves between the book pages, or create dried herbal sachets to store on your bookshelves next to the books. If your *sanctum sanctorum* has a southern exposure and enough natural light, you might even grow the plants themselves in small pots on the shelves.

*M*AGICKAL MENTION

Besides repelling paper-eating bugs, these magickal herbs have other magickal relevance:

Incense Cedar (*Calocedrus decurrens*): Protection and purification.

Mugwort (*Artemisia vulgaris*): Strength, enhancement of psychic powers, protection.

St. John's Wort (*Hypericum perforatum*): General protective powers.

Wormwood (*Artemesia absinthum*): Strong protective powers against mundane and magickal intrusion.

Shields, Cloaks, and Invisibility

To create a shield around your magickal and writing texts, begin by grounding and centering. Gather energy (from yourself or the universe), then use your hands to direct the energy over and around your texts. As you do, visualize the energy hardening into a protective blue shield. This can be done by itself or as part of a more elaborate spell or ritual. Repeat and/or upgrade as needed.

There may be times when you wish to cloak your *own* psychic nature, becoming semi-invisible so that you can slip into the background, or at least be less noticeable, e.g., when doing research or conducting observations. Here are some ways to do this:

- Using a procedure similar to that described above for shielding, harden your own auric shell into a bubble shield. Be sure to ground and center before and after.

- A simple variation on the bubble shield is the mirror shield. When forming the energy, imagine creating a mirror-like surface, off which other energies can bounce.

- Once a shield is in place, avoid making eye contact with those around you.

- Consider your attire. Subdued tones make it easy to fade into a crowd; wearing a blood-red cloak does not.

For more detailed information on the above mind-magicks, construct a magickal text or practitioner. Protection charms may also be helpful in terms of your writing and magickal texts. See Chapter 16 for details.

 _____

1. How and why might books like journals and scrapbooks—magickal or mundane—be considered Things of Power? Do you own a text that you consider to have inherent power?

2. Go to the American Library Association web site: www.ala .org. Search for and read the most current list of frequently challenged books. How many of them have you read? Set aside a page in your writer's journal to develop a list of banned books you've completed. Feel proud!

3. Install a simple bubble shield around one of your writing or magickal texts. Rejuvenate it once a month, or as needed.

eighteen

TRANSFORMING

ongratulations on reaching the final chapter! In working through this book you've encountered lessons and information about writing, from mundane and magickal perspectives. I hope that you've tried most of the exercises, for if you have, you've almost certainly seen your writing skills evolve. Now it's time to recognize your hard work and solemnize your transformation into a magickal writer. And what better way to do this than by honoring your efforts with ritual?

Ritual is at the heart of most magickal practices, and the ritual of Drawing Down the Moon is one of the best known within Pagan and Wiccan traditions. The origins of this ritual are rooted in classical times, when Witches were believed to control the moon. An ancient Thessalian tract reads:

If I command the moon, it will come down.
If I wish to withhold the day, the night will linger over my head.
If I wish to embark on the sea, I need no ship.
If I wish to fly through the air, I am free of my weight.

In the classic Drawing Down the Moon ritual, a circle is cast and some form of the Charge of the Goddess is spoken. A Priestess extends her arms to the moon and draws down its energy. If a Priest is also present, he may assist in drawing the Goddess into the Priestess. The Priestess enters a trance-state and becomes a vessel for the Goddess, who materializes as a powerful force that touches all who are present and blesses them with her spiritual powers.

The ritual is usually conducted within a circle, which becomes a sacred place through its casting—a place between worlds. Often conducted as part of an Esbat, the circle is held outdoors, usually in a private location. Within the circle the participants use music, chanting, and dancing to help raise a cone of power.

Once the power is raised, the actual drawing down begins. The evoked lunar energy can be directed toward a particular purpose or those present can simply bask in the energy until the ritual concludes.

WRITING DOWN THE MOON: A RITUAL

The ritual of Writing Down the Moon is my own writer's variation on the above. The ritual is designed to honor your work and progress; for you, it is a Rite (Write) of Passage, and it should be saved for that pinnacle moment when you are ready to declare to the world that you call yourself a writer.

Writing Down the Moon may be done as a solitary ritual or with any number of people. If possible, it should take place outdoors and on a night when the moon is full. Below is a simple outline for this final ritual—use the skills you've learned in this book to flesh out the details and make it uniquely your own.

Before you begin, ground, center, and meditate on your intention. You might want to play background music on a portable CD player: drumming, soft chants, Celtic harp music, Native American flutes, or other appropriate music.

Set up your altar as desired, including your most special pen or quill and a journal or piece of paper. Consecrate these ahead of time using the elemental means of your choice. In this ritual, your pen has male correspondence—akin to an athame or wand—and your paper represents the feminine—akin to the chalice.

Purify yourself by bathing or showering (a bar of frankincense soap is a nice touch for purification), then don clean clothing. You might also wish to purify yourself by magickal means, such as smudging.

If you have robes or garb—particularly if they are silver or white—these are ideal attire. Your writer's stole would also serve nicely. You may choose to wear magickal jewelry, particularly anything that includes moon designs or moonstones.

Create and consecrate a magickal space in accordance with your own traditions. Invoke the elemental guardians and any muses or patrons you'd like to be present. If you have others participating, you may wish to dance, sing, or chant to raise a cone of power.

At the pinnacle moment, stand in the center of your sacred space and raise your arms above your head, facing the full moon. Speak to the Goddess/energy that is the moon, asking her to fill you. Feel her energy as it flows down your arms and fills your soul. You may experience a tingling sensation, or a feeling of warmth. If working with a group, they will feel the energy as well. Most people feel very emotional at this time, and you may laugh or weep.

After you've basked in the energy, take your pen in your writing hand, and again reach both hands toward the moon. Speak to the moon again and ask her to send her energy into your pen, filling your writerly self with divine strength and power. Speak also to your patrons, if they are part of the ritual. Feel the energy as it moves from your pen—which has become a sort of lightning rod—into your body.

Moving to the center altar, drop your pen and touch it to the paper or journal, allowing the moon's energy to move from pen to paper. Spend several moments freewriting or trance writing about whatever fills you at the moment, allowing the ritual's energy to be transformed into writing. Feel the flux between you, the pen, the paper, and the moon. Feel the energy in your words. Embrace yourself as a magickal writer. Be joyous as you engage in Writing Down the Moon!

When the energy begins to subside, lay the pen atop the paper so both are still bathed in moonlight. You may wish to dance or walk the inside perimeter of your magickal space in a deosil fashion, raising additional energy. If you choose to direct the lunar energy toward another purpose, this is the time to do it. This is also a perfect time to declare a new stage and new goals in your writing apprenticeship. Enjoy feeling the energy move through you and be aware of being blessed and enriched by its presence.

While still under the full moon, celebrate with wine and cakes, or some variation thereof. If you're celebrating with others, enjoy the power of magickal fellowship.

When you're ready, release the quarters, close the sacred space, bid the elementals and patrons goodbye, then kneel and place your hands on the ground, sending the excess energy back to Mother Gaia, the primordial mother of all things, who has been with us for all time.

After the ritual, leave the pen and paper in a location where they can charge all night under the full moon—whether outdoors or in a moonlit window. Spend time meditating on what you have accomplished. Record and reflect on the entire ritual and its effects in your magickal journal.

Dearest magickal writer, it has been my great pleasure to walk with you through these pages, and to share what I know of the treasured craft we call writing. Your journey through this book ends here—but your craft as a writer is only just beginning. Treasure the path, and never stop challenging yourself to stretch just a little further. Always keep the balance of joy and responsibility inherent in the written word, and choose and use your words wisely. I wish for you a life of enchanted, writerly blessings!

 *Scribbulus* _____

1. Honor your efforts by carrying out the above ritual, or your own variation thereof.

2. Imagine a period of time over which you'd like to conduct your own writing apprenticeship. Using the materials in this book, outline an apprenticeship that involves regular writing practice and the setting of specific goals. When you have finished at least six months of work, write to me, c/o Llewellyn Worldwide. Send me a description of your process, a piece of your writing, and a copy of the certificate at the end of this book. In return, I will send you the signed certificate, marking your progress as a magickal writer.

appendix

MAGICKAL ALPHABETS

Futhark

ᚠ	F
ᚢ	U
ᚦ	Th/P
ᚱ	R
ᚨ	A
ᚲ	K
ᚷ	G
ᚹ	W

ᚺ	H
ᚾ	N
ᛁ	I
ᛃ	J
ᛇ	E/EI
ᛈ	P
ᛉ	Z
ᛋ	S

ᛏ	T
ᛒ	B
ᛗ	M
ᛞ	D
ᛟ	O
ᛜ	NG
ᛚ	L

Theban

𝔞	a	𝔦	i/j	𝔯	r
𝔟	b	𝔨	k	𝔰	s
𝔠	c	𝔩	l	𝔱	t
𝔡	d	𝔪	m	𝔲	u/v
𝔢	e	𝔫	n	𝔴	w
𝔣	f	𝔬	o	𝔵	x
𝔤	g	𝔭	p	𝔶	y
𝔥	h	𝔮	q	𝔷	z

Ogham

	B		C, K		O
	L		Q, CC		U, W
	F, V		M		E
	S		G		I, J, Y
	N		Ng		EA, CH, K
	H		St, Z, SS		OI, TH
	D		R		UI, PE
	T		A		IO, PH
					AE, X, XI

ℛESOURCES

GENERAL REFERENCES FOR WRITERS

General information on composition, grammar, and punctuation.

Davidson, George W., ed. *Roget's Thesaurus of English Words and Phrases (150th Anniversary Edition),* by Peter Roget. New York: Penguin, 2006.

> This standard text for writers will help you find the right word for any occasion.

Gordon, Karen Elizabeth. *The Deluxe Transitive Vampire: A Handbook of Grammar for the Innocent, the Eager, and the Doomed.* New York: Pantheon/Random, 1993.

> The perfect grammar handbook for magickal folk, this academic but oh-so-readable text is populated with spirits, gargoyles, and vampires! It's a great way to learn about solid writing structure.

Hacker, Diana. *A Pocket Style Manual (Fourth Edition).* New York: Bedford, 2004.

> In this spiral-bound text, you'll find every detail you need to approach virtually any writing task, as well as information on grammar, struc-

ture, academic citation, and more. This handbook deserves to be on every writer's shelf.

Pickett, Joseph P., ed. *The American Heritage Dictionary of the English Language (4th Edition)*. Boston: Houghton Mifflin, 2000.
> With hundreds of color photos, drawings, and diagrams, this dense and wonderful dictionary is just plain fun to open and read.

Strunk, William, Jr., and E. B. White. *The Elements of Style (Fourth Edition)*. Boston: Allyn and Bacon, 2002.
> The perfect book with which to start a writer's library, this one is *the* seminal text on writing well.

CRAFTING PROSE AND POETRY

Barrette, Elizabeth. *Composing Magic: How to Create Magical Spells, Rituals, Blessings, Chants, and Prayers*. Franklin Lakes, NJ: New Page/Career Press, 2007.
> Barrette gives a stellar introduction to the mechanics of writing, and in particular, writing poems and related forms.

Boynton, Robert S. *The New New Journalism. Conversations with America's Best Nonfiction Writers on Their Craft*. New York: Vintage/Random, 2005.
> A wonderful introductory text—with discussions and anthologized pieces—for those interested in literary journalism.

Gornick, Vivian. *The Situation and the Story*. New York: Farrar, Straus, and Giroux, 2001.
> A beautiful little book, written by one of the living authorities on the craft of memoir and narrative nonfiction.

King, Stephen. *On Writing: A Memoir of the Craft*. New York: Scribner, 2000.
> Two books in one! In the first half, King presents a deceptively simple course of instruction on writing; no one creates characters like Stephen King, and his descriptions here are brilliant. In the second half,

the reader is treated to a memoir of King-as-writer, complete with the chilling story of his near death after a catastrophic motor vehicle accident.

Knorr, Jeff, and Tim Schell. *Mooring Against the Tide: Writing Fiction and Poetry*. Upper Saddle River, NJ: Prentice Hall, 2001.
   A beautiful little book for fiction writers and poets. Each chapter selects a particular point of craft—voice, plot, revision, etc.—and presents both a teaching unit and an anthologized example of the form.

Le Guin, Ursula K. *Steering the Craft*. Portland, OR: Eighth Mountain, 1998.
   An "archetypal writer" of fiction and speculative fiction, Le Guin uses this text to present a course in story writing. Filled with examples and exercises, the work is fun and accessible and provides a wonderful insight into the mind of one of our most notable living writers.

Lopate, Phillip. *The Art of the Personal Essay: An Anthology from the Classical Era to the Present*. New York: Anchor/Random, 1995.
   A fabulous, thick text for those wishing to learn more about personal essay writing. A dense and detailed teaching section is followed by a rich anthology of essays, beginning with Seneca, Plutarch, and Montaigne and finishing with modern writings.

Moore, Dinty. *The Truth of the Matter: Art and Craft in Creative Nonfiction*. New York: Pearson, 2007.
   A superb overview of the three main forms for contemporary nonfiction: literary journalism, memoir, and personal essay. Each of the three sections provides a number of focused topics and a handful of story or essay examples. The end of the book includes an additional anthology for further reading. I consider this the best book available for a "nonfiction-curious" reader to learn more about the form.

Nims, John Frederick, and David Mason. *Western Wind: An Introduction to Poetry (Fourth Ed.)*. Boston: McGraw-Hill, 2000.
   In my experience as a writer and writing teacher, this is the best book I've come across for teaching the forms and methods of poetry. The

section on the importance of "sound" alone is worth the price of the book.

Rozakis, Laurie E. *The Complete Idiot's Guide to Creative Writing.* New York: Penguin/Alpha, 2004.

Don't let the "Idiots" title fool you. This text, written by a writer-professor, is a great overview of all kinds of creative writing.

Tresco, Lewis. *The Book of Forms: A Handbook of Poetics (Third Edition).* Lebanon, NH: University Press of New England, 2000.

For prospective poets interested in going further, this fascinating text takes a deeper plunge into poetic forms. Curious about terza rima, qasida, villanelle, or pantoum? This is the book for you.

Writer's Market. Cincinnati: Writer's Digest Books (published annually).

This is the bible for those writers who want to take the plunge into publication. Each year's edition features helpful instruction on how to be published and provides hundreds of pages on the available writing markets.

MAGICK AND SPIRITUALITY

Buckland, Raymond. *Buckland's Complete Book of Witchcraft (Second Ed.).* St. Paul, MN: Llewellyn, 2002.

Know affectionately as "The Big Blue Book," Buckland's lesson-by-lesson instruction on Witchcraft is entertaining, thorough, and deserving of a place on your shelf.

———. *Scottish Witchcraft: The History and Magick of the Picts (Llewellyn's Modern Witchcraft Series).* St. Paul, MN: Llewellyn, 2002.

One of Buckland's lesser-read texts, but quite fascinating.

Carr-Gomm, Philip. *What Do Druids Believe? (What Do We Believe?)* Avanel, NJ: Granta, 2006.

A solid overview of modern Druidry, as told by one of the key members of OBOD—the Order of Bards, Ovates, and Druids.

Illes, Judika. *The Element Encyclopedia of 5000 Spells.* New York: ThorsonsElement, 2004; and *The Element Encyclopedia of Witchcraft: The Complete A–Z for the Entire Magical World.* New York: ThorsonsElement, 2005.

>Illes' tome-sized books are just plain fun to read, but even more important, they are detailed, carefully researched compendiums of arcane lore and magick. Flip one of these books open to a random page and I can promise you'll learn something new.

Leland, Charles. *Aradia: Gospel of the Witches.* Blaine, WA: Phoenix Publishing, Inc., 1990. (First published 1890.)

>This seminal text on "modern" Wicca is a cornerstone of practice today, and it should be read by all magickal folks, regardless of specific tradition.

Starhawk. *Spiral Dance: A Rebirth of the Ancient Religion of the Goddess: 20th Anniversary Edition.* San Francisco: HarperSanFrancisco, 1999.

>Starhawk's text, originally published in 1979, is one of those works credited with vitalizing modern Wicca and Paganism. Her "Reclaiming" tradition served as a rallying cry for Pagans worldwide.

Valiente, Doreen. "Charge of the Goddess," as adapted by Starhawk. In: Starhawk. *The Spiral Dance: A Rebirth of the Ancient Religion of the Great Goddess (10th Anniversary Edition).* San Francisco: HarperSanFrancisco, 1989.

>Many of us recite a version of this creed on a regular basis. Here's a chance to read and consider an important version.

———. *Natural Magic.* New York: St. Martin's Press, 1975.

>Another seminal text from a woman involved in the earliest years of Gardnerian Wicca.

Walker, Barbara. *The Woman's Dictionary of Symbols and Sacred Objects*. New York: Harper & Row, 1988.

> An interesting and entertaining encyclopedic collection of arcane symbols and materials, and an important addition to the magickal library.

———. *The Woman's Encyclopedia of Myths and Secrets*. San Francisco: Harper San Francisco, 1983.

> Another work by Walker, this time focusing on myths, mysteries, and the secrets of the ages. Lots of fun to read.

Zell-Ravenheart, Oberon, and Morning Glory Zell-Ravenheart. *Creating Circles & Ceremonies: Rituals for All Seasons and Reasons*. Franklin Lakes, NJ: New Page/Career Press, 2006.

> In this wonderful text, Oberon and his extended family share traditions and rituals amassed through decades of practice. This book includes hundreds of ideas for spellwork and ritual, including basic instruction and many fully realized rituals and celebrations. For anyone who enjoys ritual practice, this book is a must.

Zell-Ravenheart, Oberon. *Companion for the Apprentice Wizard*. Franklin Lakes, NJ: New Page/Career Press, 2006; and *Grimoire for the Apprentice Wizard*. Franklin Lakes, NJ: New Page/Career Press, 2004.

> In these entertaining and eye-catching texts, Oberon—and a cast of contributors—provide instruction on a wide spectrum of magick and magickal practices. Discussions on everything from divination to tool craft to ritual to spellwork to nature studies and more are provided here, with most featuring a hands-on, do-it-yourself approach to craft. Both deserve a place on your magickal bookshelf.

BOOKMAKING, BOOKBINDING, AND ART MATERIALS

Bennett, Jim. "Calligraphy lesson—Learn calligraphy!" *Studio Arts .net*. www.studioarts.net/calligraphy/lesson.htm

Cambras, Josep. *The Complete Book of Bookbinding*. New York: Lark, 2004.

Harrison, Lorraine. *Artist's Materials: All the Materials You Will Ever Need to Make Art.* Richmond Hill, Ontario: Firefly, 2005.

Johnson, Cathy. *The Sierra Club Guide to Sketching in Nature (Revised Edition).* San Francisco: Sierra Club, 1997.

Liddle, Matthew. *Make Your Own Book Kit: A Complete Kit/Handbook and Bookmaking Kit.* Philadelphia: Running Press, 1993.

Scholastic. *Making Mini-books.* New York: Klutz, 2007.

Simmonds, Jackie. *You Can Sketch: A Step-by-Step Guide for Absolute Beginners.* New York: Watson-Guptill, 2002.

MISCELLANEOUS REFERENCES

"Bookcrossing." www.bookcrossing.com

"Encyclopaedia Britannica Online." Encyclopaedia Britannica. www.britannica.com

"Encyclopedia Mythica." www.pantheon.org/areas/bestiary/articles.html

Hare, John Bruno. "Internet Sacred Text Archives Home." *Sacred-Texts.com.* www.sacred-texts.com/index.htm

"LibraryThing." www.librarything.com

"Llewellyn Encyclopedia Website." Llewellyn Worldwide Ltd. www.llewellynencyclopedia.com

Lo, Lawrence. "Ancient Scripts." *Ancient Scripts.com.* www.ancientscripts.com/index.html

"Merriam-Webster Online." Merriam-Webster, Inc. www.m-w.com/dictionary.htm

"Roget's Thesaurus Online." Lexico Publishing Group, LLC. http://thesaurus.reference.com

GUIDED MAGICKAL APPRENTICESHIPS

A sampling of online schools and programs.

College of the Sacred Mists Online School of Wicca
www.workingwitches.com
Ages: Unrestricted for 18 and older; ages 16–17 must have parental permission; under 16 may participate with a co-enrolled
parent.
Program: Celtic Traditional and Faerie Wicca.
Tuition: see web site for details.
Certification: Certificate of degree achievement; potential ordina-
tion as priest or priestess.

Grey School of Wizardry
www.greyschool.com
Ages: 11 through adult; ages 11–13 require parental permission.
Program: Seven-level course of study in magickal practices and
general wizardry over 16 departments.
Tuition: see web site for details.
Certification: Certificate of Journeyman Wizardry.
Notes: The school neither teaches nor endorses any form of spiri-
tual or religious practice, and the student body includes stu-
dents of all faiths, magickal and mundane.

Grove of Dana Online Druid College
*http://druidnetwork.org/learning/courses/distance/druidry/dana
.html*
Ages: 13 and older; separate program for younger students.
Program: Three-level program of self-study in Druidry.
Tuition: Free.
Certification: Completion certificates.

Order of Bards, Ovates, and Druids (OBOD)
www.druidry.org
Ages: 16 and older.
Program: Three-level program in Druidry.
Tuition: see web site for details.
Certification: Certificate(s) of completion.
Notes: Some classes may be college credit-transferable.

WitchSchool
www.witchschool.com
Ages: 13 through adult.
Program: Three-degree program in Corellian Wicca.
Tuition: see web site for details.
Certification: Certificate(s) of completion.

RECOMMENDED FOR MAGICKAL ENTERTAINMENT AND ENRICHMENT

Memoir

Curott, Phyllis. *Book of Shadows: A Modern Woman's Journey into the Wisdom of Witchcraft and the Magic of the Goddess.* New York: Broadway/Random, 1999.

———. *The Love Spell: An Erotic Memoir of Spiritual Awakening.* New York: Gotham, 2006.

Essay and Personal Essay

Arendt, Elysia. *Braveheart and Broomsticks: Essays on Movies, Myths, and Magic.* West Conshohocken, PA: Infinity Publishing, 2002.

Aveni, Anthony. *Behind the Crystal Ball: Magic, Science, and the Occult from Antiquity Through the New Age.* Boulder: University Press of Colorado, 2002.

D'Este, Sorita. *HEKATE: Keys to the Crossroads—A collection of personal essays, invocations, rituals, recipes and artwork from modern Witches, Priestesses and Priests . . . Goddess of Witchcraft, Magick and Sorcery.* London: Avalonia, 2006.

Telesco, Patricia. *Cakes and Ale for the Pagan Soul: Spells, Recipes, and Reflections from Neopagan Elders and Teachers.* Berkeley: Crossing Press, 2005.

Literary Journalism

Adler, Margot. *Drawing Down the Moon: Witches, Druids, Goddess-Worshippers, and Other Pagans in America Today.* New York: Penguin, 1997.

Eisler, Riane. *The Chalice and the Blade: Our History, Our Future.* San Francisco: HarperSanFrancisco, 1988.

Hopman, Ellen Evert. *People of the Earth: The New Pagans Speak Out.* Rochester, VT: Inner Traditions, 1995.

Shlain, Leonard. *The Alphabet Versus the Goddess: The Conflict Between Word and Image.* New York: Penguin, 1999.

Wicker, Christine. *Not in Kansas Anymore. A Curious Tale of How Magic is Transforming America.* San Francisco: HarperSanFrancisco, 2005.

Nature Writing

Carson, Rachel. *Silent Spring.* New York: Mariner/Houghton Mifflin Books, 2002 (reprint).

Leopold, Aldo. *A Sand County Almanac.* New York: Oxford, 1968.

Lopez, Barry. *Arctic Dreams.* New York: Vintage/Random, 2001.

Muir, John, and Lee Stetson. *The Wild Muir: Twenty-Two of John Muir's Greatest Adventures*. Berkeley, CA: Yosemite Association, 1994.

Thoreau, Henry David and Scot Williams. *Walden: 150th Anniversary Illustrated Edition of the American Classic*. New York: Houghton Mifflin, 2004.

Williams, Terry Tempest. *Red: Passion and Patience in the Desert*. New York: Vintage/Random, 2002.

Prayer and Poetry

Mosley, Ivo, ed. *Earth Poems*. San Francisco: HarperSanFrancisco, 1996.

Pinsky, Robert, ed. *American's Favorite Poems: The Favorite Poem Project Anthology*. New York: Norton, 2000.

Roberts, Elizabeth, and Elias Amidon, eds. *Life Prayers*. San Francisco: HarperSanFrancisco, 1996.

Serith, Ceisiwr. *A Book of Pagan Prayer*. York Beach, ME: Red Wheel/Weiser, 2002.

Fiction

Bradley, Marion Zimmer. *The Mists of Avalon*. New York: Del Rey/Balantine, 2001.

Feist, Raymond. Riftwar Saga: *Magician: Apprentice* (1982 and 1986), *Magician: Master* (1983 and 1986), *Silverthorn* (1985), and *A Darkness at Sethanon* (1986). New York: Doubleday.

Hopman, Ellen Evert. *Priestess of the Forest*. Woodbury, MN: Llewellyn, 2008.

King, Stephen. *The Stand (The Complete and Uncut Edition)*. New York: Doubleday, 1993.

LeGuin, Ursula K. The Earthsea Cycle: *A Wizard of Earthsea* (Parnassus Press 1968), *The Tombs of Atua* (Athaneum Books 1971), *The Farthest Shore* (Athaneum Books 1972), *Tehanu* (Athaneum Books 1990), *Tales from Earthsea* (Harcourt 2001), and *The Other Wind* (Harcourt Brace 2001).

Paolini, Christopher. Inheritance Cycle: *Eragon* (2003), *Eldest* (2005), and *Brisingr* (2008). New York: Knopf.

Rowling, J. K. Harry Potter series: *Harry Potter and the Sorcerer's Stone* (1997), *Harry Potter and the Chamber of Secrets* (1998), *Harry Potter and the Prisoner of Azkaban* (1999), *Harry Potter and the Goblet of Fire* (2000), *Harry Potter and the Order of the Phoenix* (2003), *Harry Potter and the Half-Blood Prince* (2005), and *Harry Potter and the Deathly Hallows* (2007). London: Bloomsbury; New York: Scholastic; and Vancouver: Raincoast.

Stewart, Mary. Merlin series: *The Crystal Cave* (William Morrow 1970), *The Hollow Hills* (Stoughton 1973), *The Last Enchantment* (G. K. Hall 1979), *The Wicked Day* (Ballantine 1983), and *The Prince and the Pilgrim* (William Morrow 1995).

Tolkien, J. R. R. Lord of the Rings Trilogy: *The Fellowship of the Ring* (1954), *The Two Towers* (1954), and *The Return of the King* (1955). London: Allen & Unwin.

CERTIFICATE
⊰ OF ⊱
COMPLETION

◇◇◇◇◇◇◇◇◇◇◇◇◇◇◇◇◇◇◇◇◇◇

Magickal Writer's Workshop

◇◇◇◇◇◇◇◇◇◇◇◇◇◇◇◇◇◇◇◇◇◇

It is hereby certified that

_____

*In recognition of completing the course of exploration
and study outlined in* Crafting Magick with Pen & Ink,
is granted the title of

"Apprentice of Magickal Writing"

*Conferred on this _____ day of _____, 20 _____
with all of the rights and privileges thereof, as well as the
responsibility to choose and use one's words wisely,
and with care.*

_____

*Signed this day by Susan "Moonwriter" Pesznecker,
Professor of Magickal Writing; Journeyman Scrivenor*

CPSIA information can be obtained
at www.ICGtesting.com
Printed in the USA
LVOW08s0433041116
511570LV00007B/27/P